SECRETS IN THE DESERT

A novel

By Danna Schweitzer

Based on the short story "Light in Desert"

Originally published in the book

If God Is A Woman, Who Am I?

By Danna Schweitzer

CONTENTS

CHAPTER 1

Although I do not consider myself to be an accomplished diarist, I do feel the need to place on paper the recent events of my life. Being a man of at least a small amount of wisdom, I also hope that this will give me some sort of insight into the tale I am about to tell. Writing it all down may allow me to understand why it produces so many feelings about things I thought to be nonessentials in my own life. I consider myself, Doctor Fred Hanesworthy, to be a person of simple needs and even simpler wants but now…, perhaps I had best get on with the story and let you be the judge. I shall introduce myself with the beginning of this account.

Some weeks ago, upon leaving my last class for the afternoon, I strolled to the Student Union building on the university campus, not that I am a student, I am rather a teacher; but there is a small meeting room on the third floor used by the instructors. Most of us in the Arts and Sciences college like to gather between classes to chat without the math and business professors getting into the conversations. Rivalries and all that, you know, different thought processes. Anyway, the late spring afternoon sun was warm, the walkways relatively uncrowded as I strolled along. This is the time of year I really enjoy my life. Classes are winding down; mid-terms are well past and I find myself looking forward to the summer like one of my students.

I sometimes wonder if I have ever given up being a student. I still live within that same life-rhythm built around weekly class times interspersed with vacation periods; even though I no longer go home and sit on my mother's porch idling away a summer. For me now, summers are filled with outlines to prepare and research to be accomplished along with acting as advisor for the occasional grad student or teaching summer elective class. I also tend to avoid such things as all night drinking parties and barroom brawls. Still, being an adult in a not quite grownup world is interesting, as I was so recently reminded.

I had never intended to become a teacher, always envisioned a career in scientific research, traveling to hidden places, discovering ancient civilizations. I was born in England but came to the United States with my parents as a young child, just school age, in fact. We settled here in this small university town and set about being our version of an American family. We did not give up our attachment to England, making summer vacation a time to visit fami ly. My ambitions were formed by those early travels even though we became

American citizens as a family unit fairly early on. Both my parents are psychologists, now retired, who worked at a nearby research facility. Not a wealthy lifestyle but certainly middle-class. The choice to study locally was based on convenience both for me and my relatives, as well as the money factor. Without much fanfare, I stumbled into a position at the university before I had completed my doctoral studies and so, here I have stayed; quietly crouching behind my books and lectern, droning on about this civilization or that society to youngsters who often don't seem to care what is said as long as the grades allow them to pass their sociology exams. It suddenly hit me this day, that I had spent ten years in this manner. Something inside me groaned. These thoughts flowed through my mind as I ambled along, briefcase in hand, observing the beauty of my quiet Midwestern American campus; until I reached my intended goal.

Moving into the foyer of the old limestone building and past the elevator, I elected to take the stairs to keep in shape. Not that I am a couch- potato but as a nearly 40-year-old college professor I don't get that many chances to exercise. Up the flights, down the hall and into the room; it was spare and dark, decorated in student union leftovers for the most part since this is more of a private meeting place than one sanctioned and maintained by the university. It sits in one of the oldest buildings on campus and contains one of the few working fireplaces at the farthest end from the door. There was always something mildly clandestine about meeting here even though absolutely no one on staff seemed to be concerned about it.

The room sounded empty, or so I thought, which was unusual for that time of day. My eyes began to adjust to the low light when with the scraping of wood on linoleum, I noticed two old friends from the social studies department. The Andersens were there, finishing off a meal in little takeout boxes at a small table just opposite the door. I waved and we exchanged pleasantries. Next, I spotted an old acquaintance from an associated department, an archeologist who I thought must have just returned from a trip abroad. She was leaner and a bit tanner than when she left, in spite of it's being just the beginning of spring. She was very attractive, so I steered my way next to her just to say hello. You see, I am both healthy and decent looking for a fellow my age and since my divorce, unashamedly looking for another Ms Right. But I digress, for it is the story she told me that is most disconcerting and one that I am in such a rush to share with you now. The telling of this tale has taken the better part of these weeks and caused me to learn things about myself which I cannot easily explain.

Devon, my acquaintance from the archaeology department, is tall and blonde haired, with piercing blue eyes that seem to look right through you. Dressed in a navy-blue suit and heels, she appeared to be a bit out of place, as if she were a business executive just arriving for a meeting rather than a fellow teacher. Although younger than me by several years, she had attained her PhD over two years ago and secured a position at the university with relative ease. I understood that she was very good at research but not always inspiring in the classroom but then each of us have our strengths and weaknesses. She was standing at the far end of the room holding a bottle of water in one hand and with her attention turned toward that empty fireplace; I found I could move next to her without being noticed. Her last name gave me a perfect opening.

"Dr. Livingston, I presume," I intoned close to her ear.

She snorted a half laugh and turned her head toward me. "That, Dr. Hanesworthy is a really old line."

"Of course, it is" I grinned, "That's why I used it. How are you? Hasn't it been a while since you've been here? Someone told me you were on a quest in Europe or something"

"Yes," she flashed a smile, "I guess I have been on a journey for almost a year. I originally left on school business to work on a dig in North Africa but that led me on to a few other places." She turned as she spoke and crossed her arms in front of her which revealed a swath of bandages running up her left limb.

"Oh dear, did you get hurt?'

"Well, not on the dig" she looked at her appendage. "This first happened when we were called to a small disaster site near the work area. Earthquakes were happening and we got into a rescue situation. Actually, it's almost healed now. Not much left except the scars."

"So, gosh, come sit down and tell me all about it. My classes are done for the day and I'm up for a good story." I began steering her toward a small couch facing the picture window. The view across campus into the setting sun was quite magnificent. Green lawns trimmed by blooming bushes in red and white; trees dressed in varying shades of fresh green contrasted against the bright blue sky. I noticed then that the way the sunlight played across her eyes was quite beautiful. Devon and I had been acquainted for over ten years, since meeting through a class I taught before receiving my doctoral degree in anthropology. I was married to Helen back then; she and Devon had roomed together in their freshman year, so our relationship was casual and distant.

She and my ex-wife had not maintained their friendship after that first year in school, but they met on occasion at faculty parties. I felt at ease asking Devon to talk with me now.

The Andersens rose from their table and waved a farewell.

"We'll be in touch." Harry called from across the room.

"Of course," Devon answered, "Thanks for seeing me on such short notice."

"You call us if you need anything," Eva added in her thick British accent. Forty years in the United States and you could still tell she called another country home. "I know how trying it is to find your place again. Don't worry dear; all will work in God's favor."

Devon nodded and then glanced at me. We exchanged a smile that I assumed meant some secret knowing that we shared; although truthfully, I didn't know Devon at all. We turned then to sit and gaze into that sunlit perfect picture. It felt easier to look at the scenery than to look directly at her right now.

"The campus is beautiful this year" she stated as she scanned the panorama on the other side of the window. "What are you teaching? Any brilliant new students you're choosing to foster along through grad school?" Her conversation skimmed the surface nicely as we attempted to fit into a mental connection. I wondered if she felt as uncomfortable as I had suddenly become.

"Well, I've had the usual classes" I answered, "and no; no super brilliant students this year; just the regular motley crew of kids trying to get through before the funds run out."

"That sounds a little cynical," she laughed. "I guess you're into the end-of-the-year blahs."

"Oh," I shrugged, "I didn't think I was but I guess that was a bit snippy. Maybe my personal life is less than I want it to be right now."

"Gee, sorry to hear that." She commented. "How is Helen? Is she still teaching?"

"Actually, yes she is doing quite well," I responded all the while realizing where I was trying to lead the conversation. "We were divorced about six months ago. No big deal really, long story short we just drifted apart. I can't say it was disastrous; it was as if we both woke up one day and decided we lived in different worlds. You knew Helen, she is a great teacher and a really nice person but…"

"Did you ever have children?" she asked.

"No" I pondered aloud. "I'm grateful for that now but that was one of the troubles between us. She was desperate for them and I guess I was less so. I really still can't seem to explain it."

"No need to explain," she answered. "I thought you two were on different wave lengths even during grad school. I know you were my instructor but some of who you are comes across in the classroom."

"Really" I tried to keep the surprise out of my voice. "I never thought that would be a problem. It's a wonder no one ever told me that before."

"No one ever does," Devon said with a smile. "We can't say what will or won't work out for someone else. Besides, we were never close enough for that kind of talk." Her voice became soft and began to trail off as she continued. "If we could see what God had in store for each of us, we'd probably give up or try to talk our way out of it."

This was a new statement for my cryptic friend. Devon had been a lot of things, scientist, teacher, investigator of all ideas contained in books or the earth but not religious. I could not imagine her saying the word god outside the teaching required for her classroom. In my opinion she was the role model of a pragmatist. A bit of shock must have shown on my face because she laughed a little.

"Never thought I would say that?" she questioned. "Well, I never thought I would change the way I viewed the world."

"Really," I said; this was becoming very intriguing, "This must have been some trip for you? Tell me more."

"Oh, Freddy," she sighed once as she had settled and sipped. "Where do I start?" The intensely blue eyes flashed directly into my own and I shuddered. It was strange how she could do that, look at you as if she could see something behind your eyes. I wondered briefly if she'd ever been married, but then I remembered that her name had never changed. Women were sort of stuck that way, always having to change their names.

"Well, why not start at the beginning," I offered. "You said there was a trip somewhere, you and a crew were out of the country. I was aware that Janine Longley had gone on a site dig but I didn't know until recently that Jennifer Benson and several others were a part of that trip."

"Okay, I was on that trip and the whole thing started when we left for Africa. You know, Frank Jefferson and Janine and me, along with Jennifer and three grad students." She started. "The work site was in the hill country close to one of the smaller desert areas in Algeria, not far from the Moroccan border. The site itself had been worked for several years so we were not expecting to do more than teach the kids how to look for small artifacts. Of course, we were on a really tight schedule trying to stay ahead of the political problems over there. The politics in that country make it really difficult to get any work done some years."

As she spoke, I realized that she was talking about a rather disastrous party sent out the summer before for two months as part of a student field education class. Two of the members had come back with most of the students in time for the fall semester but some had not returned. I'd heard the story of the nonproductive work site, as many of them really are anymore, and the rush to help a nearby village, but not much about earthquakes or rescue attempts. It was odd that nothing would be circulated about that. Of course, the bulk of the gossip was about the non returning persons. Rumor had it that Jennifer and one male student had run away together.

"So," I interrupted, trying to tease, "You and Jennifer decided to become international spies for the government over there?"

"Hardly," she grinned. "I really don't know where Jennifer is now. I thought she came back with the students."

"If she did, I haven't seen her and she was working with a professor who has an office next to mine" I added, no need to get into gossip now. "Someone told me she was in Rome or Paris but I never heard why."

"Well, I don't know why Jennifer didn't return but I can share what has happened to me." She said her eyes flitting back and forth as the memories began to surface. We continued to face the sunset as the story poured out.

"We had been working along just fine when the tremors started." She continued, "They were small in our area but really early one morning there was a distress call and Janine woke us all up to go racing into the dark. We left Jennifer in charge of the three young men we were teaching, packed up a few supplies and headed out."

CHAPTER 2
DEVONT'S STORY

Bumping along a desert road in a canvas-topped jeep has never been my idea of a fun thing to do, but it was the quickest way to travel. The air was hot even though we felt like we were flying low at 50 kilometers per hour and the sun was not quite up. Miserable was the only word I could think of as I slouched down in an attempt to rest. As an archaeologist, being in the desert on a dig is the joy of my life, but this part of the trip was definitely not part of that joy.

We had been on this project in North Africa for the better part of a month when we began to experience tremors. That little shaky thing the earth does when it is trying to adjust its' outer shell. Remember how that old professor we had in geology said it was Mother Nature 'shifting her petticoat'. Anyway, it was not a town we were going to, just a location; but it seems some people there had become trapped in an old cave. This part of the world might look like a giant sand pile, but in reality, it is littered with caves and gullies, the sand often rests on top with a network of boulders in place between the topsoil and the strata of soil lower down. If the boulders shift, the sand can collapse and change the whole terrain burying any items on top.

I still was not convinced that we all needed to suspend our work but I was not in charge, Janine was acting as our department head and she had agreed to our mission in spite of my protests.

"You know, Janine, for a knowledgeable professor you sure have some old ideas. Who is this god you keep shoving at everybody? What about the most of us who don't believe in some great controller of the universe?" I was tired and no longer willing to put up with her ideas.

"I know you don't believe and I'm not trying to make you." She retorted as she popped the clutch and jerked into gear. "I just know there is a God, a Supreme Being who created us little humans and allows us to care for one another."

"So that's what you are doing," I quipped, "forcing us to run out into the desert night to help people we don't know do who knows what in the name of a deity we don't all believe in. I'm tired and cold and not happy about this."

"Be careful about your griping," She said, "when it comes to rescues, you never know who God will pick." I blew her off thinking of her as a bit of a control freak. We were closer than any authorities in the area and we did have some medical supplies as well as modern communication equipment. Irritating or not I had to admit that she was probably right in trying to help.

The jeep lurched to a stop and I opened my eyes to a rather large group of people in brightly colored robes standing around a pile of rocks on a hillside. About half way up there were swarms of people clawing at a particular spot in the rubble.

"The tremors must have closed in a cave here," Janine announced. "Frank, you radio the conditions so they know what kind of equipment to send. You, Ms. Livingston, can wake up and follow me and stop rolling your eyes." Janine loved to be in charge.

The crowd began to gather around, speaking, and motioning to the mound, so many voices, some in languages I did not recognize. This area was Berber country and the dialects could change from one tribe to the next. Suddenly, a small person wriggled to the front and spoke in very clear English "You American?"

"Yes, and we are here to help," Janine said.

"Follow me please" the person turned out to be a young woman in her late twenties. She rushed us forward through the throng explaining along the way that there was a cave, which was inhabited by a person referred to as the Ancient One who came periodically to pray in the desert, the people came to pray with him. Yesterday there had been an earthquake and the entrance to the cave had been closed. Frank began to relay the story to the Red Cross operator he had reached in the closest major city. As we walked, we heard the operator announce that a sand storm had brewed up between them and us so any rescue effort would be delayed but we were asked to go ahead with what we could.

Janine and I began to pull up rocks and rubble in the spots being worked by the natives. Janine ordered, "You take the south end and I'll help over here. Just be careful where the ground flattens out, the cave could be underneath us."

Just because she's the head of the team and a geologist does not mean that I'm an idiot. I think I know how the desert plays with you. The little English speaking girl and I set to work, when another tremor hit. I stood still and waited. Suddenly, the ground beneath me gave way and I found myself tumbling head over tail into the dark. I closed my eyes and tried to cover my head from the falling debris. I felt the sand and rocks wrapping around me and I was very conscious of fearing that I would be buried alive. Then the shaking stopped. I held my breath for a second and then opened my eyes. I could see nothing. Either I had fallen into a cave and the earth had covered me, as Janine said, or I had gone blind. At least I was still breathing and I felt no pressure on my chest although I did feel that my legs and the left side of my body were being held captive. No pain meant I had spinal injuries or I was just encased in debris either way I was still alive. "Hello," I called softly, "anybody out there".

I felt as though I was in a larger space. My right hand and arm were free so I tried feeling for something but found nothing but the dark. No walls, no rocks, no person, just empty space. I started trying to peel the rocks and sand from my body. Suddenly a voice called out, "Ouch". I stopped and listened.

"Is anybody there?" I said.

"Yes," a voice answered. "I'm here but I think I'm trapped." It was the little girl who spoke English. I was suddenly grateful for another voice.

"Okay, be careful and try not to shift too much," I instructed, "I can't see where we are but we may be in a cave or a clear space. Can you see anything?"

"No," she said and began to whimper. The crying was soft but distinct. Now I had more than just me to worry about. We must be in an open area but for how long? They would be clawing away to reach us but there was no way of knowing how much air we had or whether another tremor would crush us where we were. This was fear; I tried desperately to think of something to distract us both. Then there was another sound, it was a voice humming at first, then sounds that might have been words began. Was the little local girl singing?

"Hey, is that a song you are trying to sing?" I tried to tease.

"No, not me," she sounded even more frightened.

The voice grew slightly louder. The tune began to sound slightly familiar. The words were in a language I didn't know at all.

'Pererin wyf mewn anial dir,

Yn crwydro yma a thraw;'

"H-h-hello?" my little trapped friend spoke, "Ancient One?"

The words and accent changed but the melody and voice remained the same.

'Genade onbeskryflik Groot

Het U aan my bewys'

Now I recognized it, the voice was singing 'Amazing Grace' in Afrikaans. My friend recognized it too. She began to talk in a hushed and reverent voice. I had always been unsuccessful at learning languages so I relied on interpreters but one cannot spend a great deal of time in another country without picking up bits. My doctoral thesis was written about work I had done in South Africa so that I knew some of the words. I thought he was asking for prayers. I wondered if the rockslide had injured the old man. The voice was soothing and helped to calm my fears. Then I thought, "This is stupid, the guy is nearly buried alive and he starts singing". There is no accounting for these religious kooks.

The singing had stopped so I felt impelled to ask a few questions of my fellow cave dwellers.

"Hey," I said, "can you ask him if he can see anything and by the way, what is your name?"

Her voice came back like a smile, "Okay, my name is Tanemghurt, it means tall one in my language." She giggled at the irony. Then I heard her saying things to the other voice and that new voice answering. The conversation went on for several minutes before she got back to me. "The Ancient One says there is no light so our eyes cannot work for us. We must use our voices and our hearts to communicate."

"Oh great," I thought to myself, "stuck in the dark with a freaking old man and a mislabeled dwarf. This is how my life will end." I wondered about my life as their conversation continued. I had never been religious or consciously attended any church as an adult. I remembered a few hard fought discussions about the existence of God in my undergrad years but it was all an unnecessary mystery to me.

"Hey, American," Tanemghurt's voice broke into my thoughts. "The Ancient One wishes to know your name. He says you can talk to him straight because he can understand the language, he just can't speak it very good." It was a little broken but I sure understood.

"Okay," I started "my name is Devon. I'm an archaeologist from a University in the United States. I came here to help you get out of the predicament you are in now. My friends and I have come to help you." The voice answered in a language I still could not put my finger on then Tanemghurt spoke, "He says you were sent to him by God the Only One, to save your soul."

"Whatever," I thought, "if it pleases the old man let it be." The voices went back and forth for a minute. Then I had to speak up, immortal souls or not we were in a very tight spot and needed to have a plan.

"Hey, you two," I said in as commanding a voice as I could muster, "we need to evaluate our situation here. Obviously, we are alive now but the truth is that this whole hillside could go at any second so we need to be trying to dig our way out from inside while the folks up top are trying to work their way down. I am not in any pain so I think I'm okay but my left side and lower torso are embedded in debris. How are both of you?"

Tanemghurt answered, "I'm pretty good. I got both arms free but my left one is hurting a lot. There is something holding my feet down but I feel okay. The Ancient One only says he is where God needs him to be. He doesn't say anything is hurting for himself."

"Well," I said, "Let's start trying to unearth ourselves. I would suggest that we just sort of move things slowly so we don't disturb the rocks above us or hit one another with anything. Work slowly to conserve energy and air. No telling how long we may be here."

Slowly I began to hear the sound of stones being moved as I moved a few of my own. It felt good to release each bit and portion of my body. Then I noticed a glow, it was my own arm. My watch was faintly glowing in the dark from the energy it had drawn from the sun, dust covered everything so the glow was quite dim. This was great, at least I had some way of calculating time and now I knew I was not blind.

Within a short while, the Old Guy began to sing again, this time a melody I did not recognize. First, he hummed and then later added words of some language I did not understand and yet it was comforting. In any other situation, I would be irritated that the Old Thing was not telling us his condition or doing any more than singing. If he was free, he could be helping us free ourselves. My fears began to work on me and I started moving the stones faster and faster. Soon my left arm was free but I was covered in sweat. I had no idea how far down we actually were but the singing had ended so I decided to pick up the conversation.

"Hey, Tanemghurt," I asked "does he know how far down we are in this cave?"

The voice answered and in the next moment, she began to interpret. "The Ancient One says we are near the old entrance before the earth shook. It has been covered twice but the people keep pulling the rocks away. The cave slopes down and away very far back so there is much room if we were free to move."

That was good news. If the cave is large then we may be in a place with plenty of air and if we could just break loose from the rocks around us, we could move farther back away from the weaker formations at the entrance.

"Hey, Devon," Tanemghurt's voice came, "the Ancient One wishes to know how you believe in God."

"Uh, I don't know," this was awkward. "I never thought about it much. I don't think this is the time to worry about philosophy."

"On the contrary," Tanemghurt interpreted, "he says this is the most perfect time to reflect on life and why we are here in this place at this time."

Now I was irritated. "Just tell him to start singing"

I worked at more stones and thought about what I had just heard. It really blows my mind the way people with strong religious beliefs can expect some unseen presence to just swoop down and save them. It was not so much about the existence of some being called God; it was that they were always so insistent about how this entity could act in this real and physical world without a physical body. A thousand times I have heard about miracles that can and are easily explained by modern scientific methods. I've never seen anybody cured by anything except modern medical expertise. All that mumbo jumbo was fine for ancient people with no way to explain or understand their surroundings but in this modern age there is almost no reason to believe any religious teach-ing. It always amazed me how many young people come to the campus each year with all these ideas that some God has made them special and endowed them with gifts. Anyone with a mind can see that talents are born of genetic material and family surroundings.

All at once, I noticed that there was no singing, in fact, there was no noise at all coming from either one of them. "Hey, Tanemghurt," I said, "Are you okay? Where's the music? Tanemghurt." Silence enveloped me. I leaned my head against the cool stone and felt the tiredness creep into my body. I called a few more times but then eventually I must have fallen asleep.

Suddenly, I was jerked awake by the sound of something scratching at the stone near my hand. The glow from my watch showed a pair of insects preparing to investigate my finger. I flipped them away and checked the time. It was at least seven hours since I had last checked it. I decided to try again. "Tanemghurt." I spoke clearly, "Ancient One?"

The voice floated through the dark, "Ah Devon, you have awake. Tanemghurt is resting more." I recognized the tenor of the voice and knew it was the old guy. He knew more of the language than he let on before I fell asleep. My curiosity got the best of me.

"Tell me," I said, "How did you come to be here with these people?"

"God," The one word answered drifted back out of the black.

Then my friend spoke. "I'm here, Ancient One. My arm is very painful now. Please can you help?"

"Stretch out your arm if you can for, I am trap also." The voice continued in a strange language then ended in words I had heard before – "in Jesus' name." I was surprised. I always thought of people around here as being Muslim, but perhaps these were members of some Christian group that lived in the desert to avoid confrontation. It did not matter; the thing now was about getting out alive. I felt a bit embarrassed as though I should not be listening to the conversation but I was trapped too.

Next Tanemghurt's voice floated through the darkness "You okay, Devon? The Ancient One has pray for me and now I feel much better. He can pray for you also."

"Thanks, kid" I answered, "I've got too many other things on my mind." I tried to peer into the dark to see the place where the voices came from but the glow from the watch was deteriorating. Still no sounds from above, nothing to indicate they were trying to reach us. I wanted to give up, to say the hell with it and cry like a big old baby but that might frighten the others. How do I do anything stuck in a rockslide in the dark at what was obviously going to become my grave. I heard the old man move away from us as if he were going further back into the cave, perhaps to relieve himself. Maybe he had a secret stash of food or water.

I decided to strike up a conversation with Tanemghurt to distract us and find out some facts about what these people were even doing out here. Tanemghurt shared with me that she was born in Algeria in a nearby city but had moved to the United States to study medicine several years ago. Last year she had chosen to return before completing her studies when her father died. That accounted for her ability to translate and speak English. She lived with her mother and two younger brothers in a village only half a day's ride from the cave.

Tanemghurt explained "This is the dwelling place of a holy person we call the Ancient One. Each year for a few weeks, he comes and sits in this cave like a hermit, visiting with passersby, baptizing, and prophesying. The people of the area, some of them Amazigh, seek him out as they travel through the region. Some of us are still nomadic and travel from place to place, but most have settled into cities and lead a more modern life. No one in our community knows where he came from or where he goes when the visit is over. We do know that he is a Christian, a follower of Jesus Christ of Nazareth. He is not like the priest in my home town who preaches to all. He always talks to each visitor alone like a counselor or advisor. It is said that the Ancient One cannot die and will dwell with mankind until the end of the world when Jesus well return."

I continued to pick at the debris around me, wavering between terror at the situation and genuine curiosity at the things this young woman was telling me. My watch light was growing dimmer and the darkness became palpable.

"How is your arm? Are you cured?" The question was meant to be a tease.

"Of course, the prayers of the Ancient One are always answered by God, especially when asked for in the name of Jesus the Christ." Tanemghurt answered with very disarming confidence.

"So, just who is this Jesus Christ to you?" I was not prepared for the answer I received. The voice of the old man spoke from the darkness though I had not heard him return, Tanemghurt interpreted.

Jesus is that once living person

Person of earth and Son of Man

Jesus is Christ in his death and rising

Dying and living again in God's light

Jesus is man and Son of the Godhead

Godhead creator and light to us all

Jesus is the mirror of Yahweh

Yahweh the lover of humankind

Was this a prayer or a theological statement? Maybe it was both. I had only attended church as a youngster once or twice. There had been a few funerals, a Sunday school and a preaching service that said more about God punishing than loving. I had a roommate in college who was into the church thing and tried dragging me along to services but that was a rebellious time for me. Sitting here in a black hole with nothing else to think about I wondered at my decisions. Could I have missed something important?

"Look," I offered "I understand that those are all nice stories, the baby Jesus in a manger and giving up your life for your friends, but be honest, it is just a story. I remember the discussions in college and one person in my dorm said that the followers of Jesus made it up."

The soft voice of the old one intertwined with the singsong meter of Tanemghurt's recitation:

Perhaps we hear God's call in a wind song

Perhaps we see God's touch in a tree

Perhaps we think we do not know God

But God is our maker; that cannot be

Jesus is the Son of the Father

Searching for hearts to return to the fold

If he is false then why do men claim him?

Claim him as Savior for young and for old

Christ can arrive if we but seek him

Knock and the door shall be opened for you

Each generation must ask the same questions

Search for light that is pure and true

I continued to pick at the rocks around my body as I listened and pondered the words I heard from this ancient man through the voice of Tanemghurt. My glowing watch was dark now but somehow the sound of the two voices with me made the situation livable. It was not that I was not scared but at least I was not alone, my stomach ached with hunger and there had been nothing to drink for at least twenty-four hours. In the darkness I heard something moving toward me, I hoped it was one of them.

Tanemghurt's voice broke in, "Devon, the Ancient One comes to bring you drink."

Thank God, you might think he could read my mind. Well, probably not. After this many hours in one place, it was a natural move. Who knew he had anything to share besides words.

"Great, "I answered, "Have you got anything to eat?"

There was no answer but I felt the touch of a hard metal container on my shoulder. I grabbed it and drank not caring much what was in it. I tried not to drink too much wanting to reserve some for the others. The body that brought the flask retreated and I continued to work at the rocks. Then Tanemghurt announced that she was free and would come to help me.

"Tanemghurt," I asked softly, "ask him about all that punishment for sin stuff. Does he teach about that? That is what I remember from church. Sin and salvation, grace and damnation, those preachers could go on forever." I just wanted a little noise and distraction, or did I? Some small voice in my head called for caution, 'listen but don't believe' it hissed.

"Ah" the voice spoke with a chuckle "now we interest God's child. Is good"

Once again, Tanemghurt interpreted:

Salvation is that which makes us human

Takes us from darkness and into the light

Moves us from chaos, despair and destruction

Puts us in place with God as our love

Salvation changes the way that we view things

Humbles and gladdens our hearts and our minds

Makes us a bridge instead of a fencepost

Gives us a vision of who we can be

After that poetic statement, we worked on my encasement in silence.

In time, we heard the sound of a quiet little snore; it was the Ancient One sleeping.

Tanemghurt and I began to talk very quietly as we worked. She explained that she and her family although Amazigh in ethnic heritage, were followers of the Catholic Church. The Ancient One was thought to be a teacher from a monastery or a commune as he did not offer services or hear confessions like the priests at the church. The village viewed him as a prophet or holy person more attached to God than to any humans. He would read from the same holy book that they all used so she knew he was Christian. The most impressive thing she talked about was the way the ideals taught by the seer changed the way people acted. She told stories of people who were cruel or unkind but who changed after spending time learning from him. She told stories of miraculous healings and people becoming someone new – not just to others but to themselves as well. Life near the desert was harsh and it took the whole community working together to make it fit for human beings.

She talked of her time at the college in America where she had expected all things to be wonderful because the people had so much and how she was mistaken. She found the students often to be unkind and uncaring. For all the things they had, they seemed to lack hope. The smallest problem or trouble became a hardship over which they would give up even their own lives. She liked it better here where hope and Christianity truly intertwined with daily living.

Eventually, the rocks were all removed from around me. I was relieved and a little amazed that there were no broken bones or damage that I could locate aside from some scrapes on my forearms. I leaned back against my former prison and once again fell asleep.

Suddenly, I was jerked awake by the sound of tapping near my head. It was someone from the outside. Tanemghurt had fallen asleep beside me and the jolt awakened her. We both sat upright and listened intently.

"Do you hear that?" I whispered.

"Yes, they come for us." She whispered back.

We turned to where the tapping was the loudest and began to claw at the rocks. Suddenly another torrent of rock and sand came spilling in around us. This time we were rolled down into the cavern and landed on top of the Ancient One curled up near the side of the cave. Tanemghurt began to cry. The Ancient One began to sing. It was 'Amazing Grace' again but this time in

Tamazight. I guess it was a way to comfort all of us. Then the singing ended and we listened to the tapping at the cave entrance.

As we sat in silence afraid to move for fear of dislodging another landslide, I felt warmth within me. My mind would not focus on the tapping at the rocks. I wanted to know more about what we had been discussing. It was as if I did not want the imprisonment to end. Another part of me was arguing that it was all silliness; I was just stressed from being trapped in a cave.

"Ancient One" I addressed him directly "how do I know that this is all true? How do I figure this out?"

The voice came through the darkness very close to my face and said without interpretation, "You have begun to ask the questions. This is what is required. You will receive the answer in your heart.

To each heart a perfect answer

Perfect to that heart alone

To one who suffers pain

He is compassion

To one who is lost

He is The Way

To one who hungers

He is life bread

To one in prison

He is change

If you seek him

He will find you"

Suddenly, a light broke through. It was so bright that it hurt my eyes.

"Hey down there," It was Frank, "Anybody in there?"

We all cried out at once. There were cheers from the crowd above.

"You guys have been down there for three days," Franks face now appeared at the entrance, as the hole became larger "Who all is in there, anyways?"

My eyes began to adjust to the light. I looked about, saw two women, and then looked back at the hole. Rocks were falling but only in small amounts. Then I realized that the holy man was not there.

"Tanemghurt," I cried, "Where is the Ancient One?"

Surprised, Tanemghurt motioned "She is here." Tanemghurt pointed at the other woman, and then rubbed her eyes. Her brow furrowed as she took in the vision before her and a small gasp left her lips. The robes which normally must have shrouded her had been torn apart in the landslides. Only a thin, rough tunic covered her from shoulder to ankle.

As we rose to walk to the opening, the Ancient One looked at me and said, "Be careful about your judgments, we never know who God will pick." A rush of hot desert air hit me and I blacked out as strong hands wrapped around my arms and began to pull.

Devon stopped here and smiled. Was the story really over? There were all sorts of questions forming in my mind.

CHAPTER 3
THE MOVEMENT

The sun had set and the lights across campus were on which gave a picture postcard look to the view from the window. The sidewalks still carried an occasional shadow moving to a late class or dashing back to the dorms from the library. Devon sat staring out at the scene for a few moments before I realized she had stopped talking. It was captivating to listen to her and I really wanted to hear the rest of the story.

"Good, Lord. That's a lot of excitement. What happened next? I mean, obviously your still alive." I finally managed to say.

The eyes turned to engage me again. "I thought I had just bored you to death." She grinned. "I guess there is a lot more to the story but honestly, I need to run over to my apartment and check on some things, can I just meet you somewhere?"

"Listen," I said "It's getting kind of late here. Would you be upset if I bought you supper so I could hear the rest of this really fascinating tale?"

"Well," she answered "I was thinking more along the lines of tomorrow but I guess we both have to eat."

"Sure," I answered. "How about the Dove it serves some good food and is never that crowded during this time of year."

"Okay," she said rising from the couch. "I'll meet you there in say 30 minutes. I have a room just a block away from there."

"Ah…um, see you there," I stammered. I suddenly got a sinking feeling as if I were letting go of some important moment. "Listen, why don't you let me drive you, my car is on the other side of the campus but I could…"

"No, thanks" she waved me away as she continued to move to the entrance. "Really, I have a vehicle in the parking garage next door so it will be better if I just meet you there."

She was out the door and down the hallway before I could say more. I wondered if she really meant to meet me. "Man, you are one insecure guy." I said to no one in particular. I heard the sound of the elevator doors and began to move. I sprinted out the door and headed for the stairs. My briefcase was heavy and I mentally blamed it rather than my aging body, for my slow speed. Once I hit the sidewalk in front of Foley Hall, I was moving in a full trot, suit coat and tie waving in the wind.

I didn't see Devon anywhere as I dashed across campus and on some level, I was actually happy about that. By the time I got to my car I was totally out of breath and beginning to break into a sweat. "That's classy," I thought. "Just what any woman wants to have dinner with, a sweaty old guy who's trying too hard." The truth was I had become unsure just exactly what I wanted. She was most attractive but that story was really captivating. I put the top down on my car and hoped the moist trickles down the back of my neck would be evaporated by the time I hit the restaurant.

Driving carefully, so as not to attract the attention of local law enforcement to my slightly out of date tag, I drove out the North gate of the campus and threaded my way through the narrow winding streets. It was dark and still with just a hint of spring rain in the air. The brick streets of the old part of town broke through the asphalt in odd places causing the car to sound twice as loud as it should. I pulled into the off-street parking lot and sat quietly for a moment. Just exactly what did I expect? Was I fishing for a date, or just spending time with a rather pretty young woman? "Maybe," I thought, "and so what," I asked the face in the mirror "she accepted. We both have to eat after all."

I exited my car and headed for the door of the restaurant, a small squat building created in the early 1950's as a neighborhood grocery store, it was a place for gathering and chatting. Not a coffee house and not a bar although both caffeine and alcohol could be purchased there. The ambiance was one of adult casual dining, just the place for a good conversation. Suddenly the smell of rain triggered a subtle thought and I returned to my 1990 convertible. If it chose to rain, I was in no mood to come racing out to put up my top while my friend waited for my return. I had not held onto much in the way of personal goods when Helen and I had separated so I was not going to let the one thing we argued over be ruined by rain. Once in the restaurant, I looked around to see if Devon had beaten me there. She had not, so I requested a table near the back; I could see the door from my vantage point.

Settling into the chair, my mind began to wonder, would she show up? Would I impress her with my suave and worldly ways? Would I even figure out exactly what her angle was in this story? It almost sounded like a conversion story or the beginnings of one. I wondered if that was what had happened after she was pulled from the cave. What if she had gone on to become a follower of the lady; who sounded to me like a tribal shaman? We get into a lot of that in my work in anthropology, in my senior year I went on a trip to Central America and engaged tribes there who created whole mystiques surrounding their religious persons. That would be creepy to get involved with someone like that, especially since I'd spent so much of my life trying to avoid making a commitment in that area myself.

Seeing the Andersens in the lounge was not unusual but is sounded as if she had just finished a business appointment with them. They were affiliated with the arts and sciences college and were involved in courses that provided the history of religions in the world.   Another odd thought was about her calling me 'Freddy' no one had called me that since my grandmother passed away ten years ago. It was always Fred or Dr. Hanesworthy; even Helen never called me Freddy, for God's sake.

That was the nice thing about Helen; she never pushed about religious commitments. Her family was Quaker or Anglican or something but she stayed away from the whole church thing within our marriage. I remember a conversation between Helen and I back in those early days, we were with friends from the A&S College –Bill and Betty Something. They were both professors who taught the history of religions like the Andersen's do today. We were all discussing the necessity of religious feeling that seemed to be required for most human beings to find a sense of fulfillment in their lives. I had argued rigorously that this was hardly necessary as the very word 'fulfilled' was subjective and one should not assume that such a feeling was necessary for every other individual on the face of the planet. Bill and his wife were of the opinion that feelings that pull human beings toward belief in a deity were a part of human maturation. Helen had offered that the more 'mature' human beings seemed to be the ones who professed no such need, that instead it was those who were considered to be less evolved that fell into the god worshipping process. It turned into quite a discussion that night.

My reverie broke apart as Devon entered my range of vision. She really was quite pretty. I had thought of her as sort of masculine and linear before, but she didn't seem that way now. She had changed from the suit she had been wearing in the lounge to a casual pair of slacks and a white shirt. The bandage seemed to be absent under the long sleeves. I rose to meet her as the waitress brought her to the table.

"Hi", she said with a grin. "Hope I haven't kept you waiting long. I decided to find something more comfortable to wear.”

“No”, I said. “Not long at all. I haven't even had time to order yet.”

The waitress left menus this time and we began to look things over as we stole nervous glances and created small talk. “So how is the food here?” She began. “I don't think I've eaten here since I was an undergrad.”

“Oh, my,” I responded. “Well, it's not bad. The fish is all good and the chicken is okay but I would stay away from the beef. They say it's less than perfect.”

She smiled. I offered one of the questions I'd been dying to ask

“When I saw you earlier at the lounge, was I interrupting a meeting …?”

“No actually,” she sighed perusing the menu, “I was asking for a job for next year. After my ordeal with the cave-in, I had requested a sabbatical and now I want to go back to work.”

“Oh really,” I said. “I figured it would be pretty automatic unless they had filled your position.”

“No, not really,” she answered then changed the subject. “I think I'll try the salmon. It sounds good. Are you teaching this summer?”

“Yes,” I tried to go with the flow which seemed to be going in several directions at once. “I'm doing a short intensive on the history of the Hopi tribes in America. It's a fairly popular elective.”

“Sounds interesting,” she answered. “I'm looking at teaching some really basic classes for the fall if they have me back. I wasn't planning on missing out this summer but I'm really too late to pick up a class now.”

“Well, I could put in a word for you if you thought it would help,” I offered, “I can't say I have any big influence but I don't think I've created any enemies yet. Of course, you were talking with the Andersen's and that's not in my field, or yours either if I remember correctly.”

She smiled and sipped her water but made no further comment. The waitress appeared next to us with an expectant air. “Are we ready to order? The chicken almond is really good tonight.”

We ordered and sat taking in the atmosphere of the room for a moment. Smiling awkwardly from time to time, and fiddling with the napkins and tableware, it was astonishing that we had suddenly lost the connection that had felt so magnetic less than an hour before. Was she waiting for me to ask another question? Where was it that she had stopped before?

"Was everything okay at your apartment?" I asked.

"Oh, sure," she said, "just checking for phone messages, the teaching position and all that." Her voice trailed off for a moment. I waited knowing there would be something else.

"Fred," Devon began "are you at all religious? I'm not being nosy but I think you can tell by the beginning of this story that it will have a lot to do with religious belief. Is this even something you want to hear about?"

I hesitated in light of my own internal questions. "Truthfully, I can say that this is not a subject I have feelings about one way or the other. My work in anthropology has taken me in lots of different directions over the years and I have learned of the teachings of most of the world's religions. I don't have a personal belief so I think I can hear your story with an open mind."

"Can you understand that this may become very personal for me and that my sharing this story with you is actually difficult?" She looked as though she needed to be heard.

"I do respect your feelings" even I thought that one sounded trite. "Perhaps this started out as just an adventure tale but I have the idea that more is involved. I hope you can trust me with what you are going to say." There that didn't sound so bad.

Devon hesitated again and then began where she had left off.

CHAPTER 4
TANEMGHURT'S TALE

As I said when we last spoke, I blacked out as we began to exit the cave so I don't really know what happened but I woke up in a hospital in Rabat, Morocco being waited on by several very nice nurses. I had been fortunate that no bones were broken but the sand and stones that wrapped around me had shredded both my clothing and my skin. That's part of the reason I still have to have some bandaging done from time to time. There are salves required to keep my skin clean and moist.

The Rabat hospital was very tidy but, in the beginning, I was on so much pain medication that I really don't remember a lot. The days and nights swirled together for a while, although I remember Janine and Frank coming by to check on me once. They said they had returned to the dig site shortly after I had been mediflighted out of there; they had found Jennifer and the kids in good condition, but they had taken a vote and decided to head back to the states a few weeks early as the earthquakes seemed to continue and the site had not provided any new information. Those few days left alone in the desert with the possibility of raiding nomads and unfriendly government workers was just too much for all of them. You know, I don't remember feeling fearful of things before all this happened but I could understand their trepidation now. They left my personal belongings with the hospital staff and made sure I had credit cards available to help me get home.

When I did finally come to and begin to piece things together, I found I could not get the words of the Ancient One out of my head. The image of her standing there haunted me and not just because I was mistaken about her gender. She was only about four and a half to five feet tall and rather thin. I got a glimpse of wispy, white hair and the most piercing brown eyes you could imagine. Her complexion was very dark and her features more South African than the local population. I dreamt of her and thought about her and my little interpreter Tanemghurt. I guess I felt I should have been worrying about my job or the expedition we had been on but that's not where my mind would go. None of the nurses could tell me where they were or if they had been injured and I had not had the presence of mind to ask Janine what had happened to them. It was as if they had vanished from the earth. Of course, they were Berber or Amazigh as they call themselves and there is a real prejudice against them in Morocco.

Then on the third week that I would spend in that hospital I got a visit from Tanemghurt and a tall, thin gentleman. They had been looking for me at hospitals in Algeria and had not been able to locate me until a friend of hers at a local University got word to her that I had been moved to Morocco for my own safety. They had traveled for over a day to reach me in Rabat. On this day she was wearing the traditional clothing and hijab or veil which hid all but her eyes. She removed her facial cover once they were seated and we were fairly sure we would be undisturbed. I was certainly glad to see her but also disappointed that the Ancient One was not with her. The man who accompanied her turned out to be her brother; a woman with a Berber name traveling alone was in certain danger in that part of the world.

We sat for awhile chatting politely about our experience in the cave, she said she was fine, that the healing by the Ancient One was complete and she required no other medical attention.

"Tanemghurt," I asked, "why were you cured and yet I am still injured? Why didn't the Ancient One cure me as well?"

"Because you did not ask," She stated in a matter-of-fact tone. "The work of healing can only come if we ask; although God may know that you need healing, God will not offer unless you ask."

"So, tell me" My curiosity got the better of me, "did you know that the Ancient One was a woman. I could swear I heard you say 'he' when referring her."

Tanemghurt seemed to smile briefly and her brother, who reported to be unable to speak English, shuffled in his chair. "For long centuries there has been an Ancient One and it was always believed to be a man. Always the Ancient One comes to us in long robes with a hood that will guard against the desert sun and hide the eyes from the sting of sand. The truth is that we do not know and now the God that we love has given us a vision which we have come to worry about very much. My brother and I come to ask your help in our time of trouble. We need to find the Holy One and we are unable to do so on our own. We believe you can help us once you are well again?"

I was taken aback but not really shocked. The time I had spent in the dark with Tanemghurt and the holy woman had awakened something within me that seemed to call me to another place in my heart. The request they made was both intriguing and somehow welcome. We continued to talk as she explained all that had occurred following my blackout as the rescuers reached us. My collapse had naturally brought all the attention to me which had allowed the third member of our party to escape in the confusion of the crowd. Tanemghurt shared that only one small boy had actually witnessed the Ancient One leaving the cave and walking away across the sand dunes. My memory of her was the elderly woman in a thin torn tunic and I wondered at her ability to survive in such a hostile climate.

Tanemghurt stated "You were loaded into the vehicle in which you had arrived by the other members of your party. They had started to drive away to find more medical help when a helicopter was seen over the horizon." The sand storm had evidently subsided and the International Red Cross had been sent out from the Moroccan side of the border in search of whatever might be found.

"The medical chopper landed and loaded you, unconscious, into a side pod" Tanemghurt continued. "The big lady," (this had to be Janine) gave all the necessary information to the medical team and received some information back." That's how she and Frank had been able to see me on their way back to the University. Janine had stayed with the people of the cave site for a few more hours making sure that Tanemghurt was well and briefly helping them look for the Ancient One. Then she and Frank crawled back into the land rover and drove away.

My new guide continued, "The people who had been gathered began to filter away from the site. At first there had been some questions about continuing to look for the holy person but it very quickly became clear that the vision of the Ancient One we had all witnessed was disturbing. A few of the women seemed pleased that the person was one of us but most just felt astonished and overwhelmed. There was talk of searching but there was also a feeling of not wanting to know anymore. If the Ancient One was not who they expected, did that mean that all the other stories and traditions were also false? Some of the people packed up their families and left the area on whatever form of transportation they had brought. Many remained and began to build campfires preparing to spend one more night in the area so that leaving could begin at dawn. The tremors had subsided in the area and an air of calm began to return to the encampment. It was following the evening meal that the stories began."

"Idir Imiran, an elderly man who had traveled from the area around In

Salah, began by saying that he had often wondered if the stories concerning the Ancient One were not a bit exaggerated, that perhaps there was more than one person taking on this role. This, of course, caused a cry of anger among the others. It was disbelief and could not be tolerated. Our people depend upon the stories of the past to tell them how to face the troubles they will find tomorrow. The story was repeated that the Ancient One would not see death until the second coming of the Christ."

Tanemghurt stood and began to pace as she spoke, "I was then brought forward. As I had spent three days in dark with you, the scientist and the Ancient One, surely, I would know who this was and what had transpired. I did share the story that I knew about the words of the holy person in the dark and how I had translated from Tamazight to English in spite of my pain. Then I shared the story of the healing of my arm and how the touch of the Ancient One had caused this to happen. Finally, I had to admit that I did not much care if it was a man or a woman; that with the healing, it was faith in the God we had all learned to love that counted. The crowd stood silent and pondered my declaration."

Tanemghurt had not known that some of the languages the Ancient One spoke were Afrikaans and a Germanic dialect that none of us could understand. Her talent in those days in the cave lay in her knowledge of the languages we used to communicate with one another. She was unaware of the clues that lay in the languages sung by the prophet. The people gathered around the campfire were Amazigh by birth and Christian by choice. Their Amazigh heritage could make them almost too proud to accept this person no matter how holy Tanemghurt or her community felt that person was. She did not like the feelings she sensed from the gathering as they struggled with the issues of gender bias. Her years as the eldest daughter of her Amazigh parents had taught her many things and one of them was to hold silence and wait.

Isaac Rahashid, a Taureg from the Tindouf region, offered that perhaps they were all mistaken in what they thought they saw; perhaps it is not a woman at all.

"The person is quite old and the body changes with time. We probably just thought we saw a woman's figure." The gathering approved of this idea and several of the older men and women laughed and agreed that body changes most certainly happen to old people. Then a woman within the crowd rose to offer a suggestion.

"Bring the boy," she said, "He was last to see the Ancient One. We must ask him for his observation for he is young and innocent. He will tell us what is true." The assembly agreed at once and the child, a six-year-old boy, was roused from sleep and brought to the circle. Sacred Scripture was brought to mind with shouts of "and a child shall lead them" and "Out of the mouths of babes the Lord will speak".

The child, a small one for his age, stood in the circle rubbed his eyes and faced Idir Imiran who had assumed the place of leadership in the crowd. Idir ordered silence with the raising of his hand,

"We must not frighten him. Where is his father?" Idir declared. The father came forward timidly at first but when Idir indicated that he would be moral support for the boy and that no person would hold him responsible for the boy's answers, the man relaxed and took his son's hand.

"What is the child's name?" Idir asked.

"It is Izri, after my father." The young man said proudly

"Tell me, my child," Idir began in his best soothing voice as he knelt to speak, "today when the persons were coming out of the cave, what did you see?"

"I see the people. I see a people that fell down and they bring it up from the rocks asleep." The little person spoke clearly, his eyes wide with wonder.

Idir smiled. "Yes, very good and what else did you see."

The boy began to relax, "I see the lady" he pointed at Tanemghurt.

The crowd smiled and nodded. "I see the other one. It came up out of the rocks by itself."

"Yes," Idir nodded "And what did you see the other one do."

"It went the other way," he said. "It goes that way." He pointed toward the desert.

"Yes," Idir urged "tell me, Izri, did you notice if these were men or women?"

"The sleeping one was a man." Izri replied wrinkling his brow as if deep in thought. The crowd moaned. Devon had been dressed for her work in khaki pants and shirt with boots on her feet; compared to the women the child saw on a daily basis, she probably did appear quite manly. Perhaps this was not the answer. "The others were also men but from our tribe, I think."

Idir looked disappointed and rose to his feet. "Very well, Izri," he could not blame the boy after stating that the child would know the truth. "Perhaps the child is too tired to continue."

Suddenly the boy's father spoke, "Izri, tell what the last person did that was different. You told me before that the last one was different."

"Yes, Papa" Izri looked up at his father who continued to hold tightly to his hand. "The last one move but did not walk. I think it has no legs."

"The crowd was stunned," Tanemghurt continued her words flowing as she grew into the excitement. "More questioning followed after which it was determined that the Ancient One had 'floated' out of the encampment. The vision the crowd now faced was that the holy person had risen from the cave area and been born away by God as if by some invisible force. For them this became further proof that the Ancient One was indeed, a man. After all, was not Jesus a man, a man who died but was raised by God from the dead? Perhaps then the Ancient One had died in the cave and was now raised to heaven to abide with God. The stories began to surface about miracles and cures attributed to the Ancient One and how blessed they all were for having been present to witness this great miracle. Then it was remembered that the Ancient One was not supposed to leave until Christ returned. They began to wail and cry, grasping at one another and looking to the heavens."

"Words flew into the still desert air and reverberated among the rocks," her gestures became larger as her story emerged. "How could God do this to us? We have not finished living, our children with so much promise and how shall they fulfill their lives? Suddenly a very elderly man stood and raised both his hands for silence."

It was Azerwal Mashneh-Amed of the nearest province and one of the oldest visitors to the cave. "While it is true," he announced with great ceremony, "That we have witnessed great things in these days, are these things the proof of our faith in our God? When the great Lord Jesus Christ left the apostles to return to the Father, did they remain forever to cry and rend their garments or did they go off under the blessings of the Holy Spirit to offer the 'Good News' of Gods' love to their neighbors? Do we worship the Ancient One or do we worship the One God?" The crowd grew silent again. They would have to ponder this in private. The end of the world did not seem near. Azerwal Mashneh-Amed turned toward his tent. The men and women began to filter away and the fire was damped down in preparation for the night.

As Tanemghurt finished this part of the story a young nurse appeared at the door. Her excited voice had begun to draw the attention of some of the hospital staff. The medical person checked my vital signs and seemed to need to assure herself that I was not in danger from this foreign woman so I tried to indicate that both Tanemghurt and her brother were my long-lost friends. Thankfully the story stopped until the nurse was called to another room. Then my new friend continued.

When Tanemghurt and her family rose in the morning some had already left the encampment, no longer willing to question or listen to stories. There were problems but the answers that were available seemed so terrible that no one wanted to ask them anymore. Tanemghurt's brother, Fadil, a twenty something year old who sat quietly in the chair across from my hospital bed, was still concerned that morning and stopped by the tent of Azerwal to see what other insights he might have for them.

At the entrance to the tent Fadil stopped and asked a young woman coming out if Azerwal was available before entering. She indicated he was and held open the tent flap for him to enter. Bowing low as a sign of respect, Fadil moved to the center of the area indicated by the neighbor's wife and sat cross-legged at the small round table. Fadil was young but had been well brought up by his parents and so knew the proper Amazigh way to present himself before others.

"Mr. Mashneh-Amed," he began as Azerwal entered and seated himself, "how are you and all of your fine family?"

"We are quite well, in spite of our recent upset" Azerwal answered. "How may I help you?"

Fadil began, "I am here this fine morning to try and ask you a few questions without all the others present so that I might help my family in making some further decisions."

"You are quite a sensible, young man. Please continue." The old gentleman was impressed.

"We have traveled far to be here," Fadil began "my mother and sister and brother. Our father died some years ago in the market square so we have only ourselves to rely on."

Azerwal was impressed by Fadil that such a youth would be willing to come as a man to seek the counsel of an elder. He would listen as the family situation and short history was explained. This was the proper way for a young Amazigh to approach another man. Obviously, he would be treated with respect and no question would be thought improper. Fadil sought the story of the Ancient One, how the legends came to be and where the Ancient One came from as he was only seen at the cave for the one month out of each year. Fadil could remember no year when his family had not come to the cave to pray and seek counsel.

Azerwal related the story of a young monk who had been sent to school in Spain in the early centuries before the ban on Christianity. He returned to a monastery at Beni Abbes before the Muslims took over the running of this part of the world and the lands of the Amazigh. The young monk was very wise and from time to time was granted permission to go out into the desert for prayer and solace, a time of silent retreat with the Lord. On one particular trip to the desert cave a storm blew up and a caravan of traveling Amazigh sought refuge in the cave occupied by the young monk. Although he was seeking silence, he would not turn the caravan away into the storm and made them welcome. The storm was long, lasting five days and four nights, which gave the men time to talk and share their stories.

Early in the morning of the second day of the storm one of the caravan members became very ill. It was fever and at first, he was tended to by his fellow travelers. The monk continued to see to the needs of the caravan as they waited for their friends' illness to subside. Late in the afternoon of the third day of the fever the monk asked if he might be allowed to pray for the young man. Although the caravan consisted of followers of the old gods of the desert, they had become desperate and agreed to allow the clergyman to pray to 'his god'. The monk bent over the man, placed his hands on his head and prayed the prayers of healing. Immediately the young Amazigh sat up and began to praise God. The members of the caravan were amazed and asked the monk to tell them all about his faith and his God. Even though the storm had subsided they were so impressed that they chose to remain near the cave and the holy man. He shared much of his story about Jesus Christ and the teachings of the Catholic Church. Two weeks later came the time for them to depart. The monk gave directions to the Catholic Churches in the city they were journeying to and then wrote a letter to be given to the bishop at that church telling of the tale.

The story of the healing spread throughout the region and by the next year when the young monk returned to the cave a number of people came for healing. Along with the healing, the monk would talk to them about believing in the one God and Jesus Christ and then he would baptize them. As the years came and went the crowds grew and the priest aged but still returned to the cave. One year, when Azerwal's 8th great grandfather's grandfather was a boy, the monk arrived with a helper. He explained to the crowds that he was growing older and closer to the time that he would go live with the Father in heaven and then he would see them no more. The cry and wail that rose from the crowd on that day was enormous. How would they be healed? How could they continue to learn of the Lord Jesus Christ?

The monk and his companion consulted and prayed for several hours that day. In the evening as the sun was beginning to set over the sand dunes they emerged from the recesses of the cave and made their announcement. There would continue to be a monk from the monastery for as long as the people had need of such a presence. They were urged to attend to the churches in other cities and continue to learn from the preaching of their village bishops but the monks would continue to come to them until Jesus the Christ returned. The years wore on and the world changed. The monk continued to come each year. The way of the Church changed and bishops began to be aided by priests who stayed with the people. The monk continued to come each year. Then the teachings of Mohammed began to filter through the countryside and wars raged. Still, the monk came each year. It was even said that the monastery at Beni Abbes was destroyed and yet the monk came. Even today as the Amazigh begin to leave the ways of the desert, still the monk comes. It was never asked who the monk was, only accepted that each year there was a monk.

At the end of the story Azerwal and young Fadil sat in silence for a time. The enormity and the truths of the story were not wasted. That this was all one person now seemed less certain.

"I beg of you, sir," declared Fadil, "have you never shared this version of the story before now?"

Azerwal shook his head and with clear blue eyes staring out at the desert dunes explained how his family had always held this story in their hearts being careful never to undermine the belief of those who came here to worship. He had thought about it in his youth but a counsel with the Ancient One had helped him change his mind.

"For many people," Azerwal said, "the thread which ties them to their faith is as thin as a spider web. If left undisturbed it may grow into a strong, fast cord that cannot be broken by thoughts or stories; but for others," Azerwal sighed, "they never seem to grow. The Ancient One shared that this is the work of God and we must be careful not to stand in God's way."

Fadil said no more but thanked Azerwal for his kind words and for trusting him with the truth they had shared. He returned to the tent of his family which was nearly ready to go home, packed the last of their things and said nothing until they were back home in Adrar. As evening approached, he finally sought out his big sister Tanemghurt and shared the story with her.

"Fadil," I asked, "why did Azerwal share this with you if it is such a grave secret? Truly it must be a serious secret for this is not what the people believe."

"He said that he has no sons and therefore will not be able to pass on his legacy in an appropriate manner." Fadil was clearly upset. "Azerwal is quite old and does not expect to live out the year. He is a good man Tanemghurt; I don't believe that he is lying."

"We sat together on a bench at the entrance to the home we shared with our mother and youngest brother." Tanemghurt continued her story as she paced my hospital room. "Should we do something with this information? Was it even our place to meddle? We are both in our twenties, old enough to work and support the family but not quite old enough to handle adult matters when they deal with subjects of such enormity. We decided to visit with the local priest when he came to say the weekly Mass at the little chapel. Surely, he would know what to do."

"Two days later we sat in the small chapel room waiting for the priest to meet with us." Tanemghurt sounded sad as her story continued. "We had hoped to see him before the service but he had been delayed by police on the way in to town and had arrived nearly two hours late. It is very difficult to be Christian in an Islamic world," she sighed.

"Finally, the priest came and sat next to us on the bench. No other persons were present in the chapel so we were able to tell our parts of the story in succession. All through the story the priest continued to shake his head and appear incredulous. Once we had completed the tale, he told us, it seemed fantastical and in reality, he had only heard of a faith healing monk in the country, he thought it was just another Berber folk tale. The old priest said he did know about a hermitage at Beni Abbes but that it was not a place for us to go meddling into. He scolded us for telling such tales and following a false god. Next, he told us that he would certainly pray for us but there was nothing he could do as this was outside his territory and he had to be on his way before nightfall. We understood his dilemma and left without knowing any more than when we had come."

"It was on the drive home that I began to form the plan to find you and ask for your help." Tanemghurt turned to face Devon with a soft stare in her large brown eyes. The three days in the dark in the cave had not only cured the injury to her body but had forged a kinship between us that allowed us to know one another without words. We had shared so much during those dark hours about our lives and hopes and dreams, the past and the hoped for future. Tanemghurt was positive that I would come to their aid.

Now sitting in the hospital room and looking at me, tears sprang to her eyes, "I beg you Ms Devon, for help in finding the Ancient One. I cannot say if the stories are true or false but I must find some facts for the sake of the faith of my family." At that moment Tanemghurt was torn between devotion to whoever was responsible for the cure of her own body and a feeling of being fooled, told a story that could not ever be true. Something within her warrior heart could not let the people go without some knowledge of the truth. Fadil remained only to protect his sister.

They left the hospital without an answer to their questions but with the promise that I would consider what they had been telling me. At that point I was still not quite well and could not tell them when I would be available to discuss their dilemma.

I waited several days before coming to any conclusions myself. I was under no obligation to take up their quest but the thoughts and dreams of the conversations in the dark of the cave haunted me taking over my mind. I felt as if I were being forced into an area, I knew nothing about.

CHAPTER 5
THE STORM

Once again, I had been caught up in the story as Devon unfolded it. We had finished our meal and I thought we would have to leave. I searched for a reason to remain listening to her account. Outside the gentle mist had turned into a rainstorm so we decided to stay for a while to see if the tempest would subside. As the waitress stood poised to receive our coffee order, the little eatery was rocked by the sound of a huge lightning strike followed immediately by thunder. The lights of the establishment blinked twice and then we were plunged into darkness. I felt Devon grab my hands and we held on for a moment. There was the sound of pandemonium in the kitchen area, the manager emerged with a flashlight and asked the patrons not to panic. Another gentleman dressed in white came in and announced that lightning had hit a power station a block away; it looked as though a fire had started but this building was safe.

It was late enough that we and one small family were the only customers left. On each table was a small round globe containing a lighted candle, something that was lost with all the lights on, but now the candles saved us from total darkness and our decision to ride out the storm here seemed more than appropriate. Sirens began to wail in the distance as the downpour continued. Calm began to return and Devon let go of my hands, now seemingly embarrassed at her action.

"Sorry" she mumbled.

I smiled into the dim light.

"Thanks for grabbing my hand there. That was rather terrifying." I spoke.

The young family in one of the booths near us decided to brave the weather, shoved some money at the manager, wrapped a child in the gentleman's jacket, and exited in a hurry. Another crash of thunder set the child screaming as they ran for their vehicle. We were left with the servers and the manager. A new waitress brought two cups and a carafe of hot coffee along with a complimentary dessert from her supervisor.

"We are so sorry," she spoke with a Southern drawl as she poured. "We hope this won't last very long but who knows. These thunderstorms brew up outta nowhere."

"I'm sure we will be fine" I smiled, "This coffee is very good."

"Well, you folks just take your time. Jenny, your first waitress had to leave but I work to close so I'll be right over there if you need anything, y'all just holler." She flashed her toothy grin at us and walked toward the cash register. Within the next few moments, she was joined by several more members of the kitchen crew. They all came out into the dining area where the candle lights flickered in the darkness, but remained a respectable distance away as if choosing not to interrupt. Several took up coffee cups and seated themselves at a far booth.

"Please go on" I urged her "I think your story will get our minds off the storm."

"Are you sure?" she said. "I'm not convinced I can do this for an audience." Devon nodded toward the small gathering of personnel.

"It is beginning to sound very personal."

"What about your family?" I interjected to lighten the subject. "Your parents or siblings, how did they take the news of your injuries?"

"Well, all I really knew I had was my mother; she was a research scientist with Global Pharmaceuticals living in London. I left a few messages for her and eventually received a card." Devon gazed away into the dark. "Saying we were not that close is an understatement."

I had thought to take her hand again but somehow it seemed inappropriate to the story. Instead, I caught her gaze and sent a reassuring smile.

"No other family or friends or boyfriend?" I fished.

Devon smiled "No, I had been dating a guy but that ended before we left on the trip. I guess my agreeing to accompany Janine was based in part on the need to get away from that relationship."

Again, I smiled, reassured that I was not trespassing.

"As for family," she mused "it was really only mother and me at the time. My parents divorced when I was about three, and she and I lived with a friend of hers for a couple of months. At some point before I started school my father had remarried and I was sent to live with him in a small town in Kansas. Mother wanted to attend graduate school and I suppose was getting to be a problem for her. Dad and Shelly, my step-mother, had a set of twin daughters when I was in second grade, Kelly and Kristi. They were a pair of devils some days but they were my sisters and we really had a pretty good life."

Suddenly I caught the verb she was using, "Had a good life?" I asked.

"Yes," her voice dropped. "When I was a junior in high school, my dad and sisters were killed in a car accident on the way to pick me up from a basketball game." This time I did reach for her hand but she recoiled. "It was pretty devastating for me at the time but I've grown since then. I have to admit that relationships are often difficult but I muddle through."

"That is a tough break." It was the only comment I could come up with but I thought to myself "what a brave little person."

"Well," she continued "I had a good life with my dad and sisters, all the usual things you hear about nice families. When they died, I had spent enough time with my step-mom that it didn't feel too weird to stay with her, most people in the town where we lived had forgotten that I had another mother somewhere. When I graduated from high school my mother came for the ceremony and somehow, she and Shelly decided I should go to live with her while I started college. That's really how I ended up here at the university."

We sat in silence for a few moments listening to the rain. I wasn't sure how to proceed without seeming crass or uncaring. Then she broke the quiet with a question.

"How about you, Fred?" she squinted as she spoke "What would be a quick synopsis of your life? I know you were born in England and came to this country with your family…"

"Right, well" I scrambled for the memories "I was born in Cambridge actually. I have an older sister and a younger brother, both of my parents are still living and; as you said, we all live in this country, each in our own homes or apartments. Can't say that it's a happy little family though, a lot of quarrels and arguments. Not bad people just lots of diverse personalities, I suppose."

"Sounds like a fun group to me," Devon smiled and cupped her hands under her chin. "I bet you are the peace maker among your siblings."

"Now that you mention it, I suppose I am." I had to grin at that as I half remembered the last family gathering. "We tried spending Christmas Eve together this last year and it was rather a disaster. My brother and sister had decided to travel in the same vehicle but then got into a row over some small thing and both ended up taking a taxi to their respective homes. Mum and I tried to return the car to my sister's house later that day only to discover it was my brother's auto. It was a bit of a mess."

We shared a giggle between us and the silence set in again. I tried to think of something else to say but the story of Devon's adventure kept calling me. I had to get back to her account.

"Are you ready to return to your latest adventure, Devon?" I offered, leaning in to catch her eyes. She smiled, took a long sip from her cup and continued without further comment.

CHAPTER 6
THE SEARCH

Within a week I was released from the hospital in Rabat and found a room in a local hotel. From there I called the University here and received verbal permission to take a sabbatical which I offered would only last until the spring classes would start. I certainly didn't share any of my conversation about the holy woman but let them think it was a need to de-stress after the ordeal in the cave. They said they would have to take it up with the board but as it was summer, and since Janine and Frank had already returned with news of my injuries, they could not foresee any difficulty.

Anyway, that gave me almost three months to locate the Ancient One and try to get some answers for myself. It wasn't that I owed anything to the Berber people at the cave site but I did feel an allegiance to Tanemghurt. Of course, there were those pesky questions of my own that kept rolling around in my head. Really who was this Jesus Christ? Why was the life and death of one presumed historical figure so important to most of the civilized world? One cannot complete an education without hearing about religious beliefs but I had always placed them in the same category as historical facts and social mores of other civilizations or at the very least, other people. I'd never been inside a Catholic Church much less visited with a priest or a monk or whatever that person was. Still, her poetic explanations crawled through my mind from time to time; a strange occurrence for me.

Traveling alone in this part of the world can be dangerous for a woman, especially an American tourist. Morocco is an Islamic country and all the rules apply as far as dress and conduct in public. As long as I stayed in Rabat, which is a tourist town, I knew I was relatively safe but I needed some allies to go very far; the fact that I was searching for a Christian group in a country where you could still be persecuted for your personal beliefs did not help my case. Tanemghurt and her brother had left me several phone numbers to try and reach them so I secured a local cell phone, made some calls, and then found the nearest library. We had come with the clothing necessary to leave the desert and travel into Islamic cities so I was prepared. Now I needed to know a lot more about Beni Abbes and the religious order I might be dealing with.

It took only an hour for Tanemghurt to answer my call. She and her brother were still in Rabat staying with relatives, she met me at the library two blocks from my hotel and we began our search. Fadil was not as interested in our project but once again was willing to tag along as protection. The library was not open very late but we were able to commandeer a small study space which allowed us to talk quietly as we began to pour over old books in the reference section. Most of the books were in Arabic so having Tanemghurt and her brother along was essential.

In that first meeting we were able to understand that there was indeed a hermitage at Beni Abbes in Algeria not far from the cave site. It was operated by the Little Brothers of the Gospel, a fraternal order of Roman Catholic priests. The hermitage was occupied most of the year so there was a chance that we could contact someone there.

"We should try to call someone at the hermitage," Tanemghurt said. "We may be able to visit them and find out more."

"Even if we do," I said skeptically, "do you know the actual name of the person who was at the cave? Who do we ask for if we even find this monastery?"

Tanemghurt answered confidently "That will not be a problem for I am quite certain that any person with such great gifts as healing would be well known among the community. Surely, this person is very much honored and revered?"

"I don't know," I shook my head "this could all be a wild goose chase." I was not ready to believe in miracles. I didn't see my friend's injuries in the cave that day. A simple muscle pull or bruise can feel every bit as painful as a broken bone when a person is frightened. What if we had all been fooled by some poet speaking words in the dark?

The library was closing so there was no time to check out any of the volumes we had been perusing. Besides, the curious stares and suspicious looks of the librarians were beginning to make me feel uneasy. Fadil seemed to notice the attitude also and motioned for us to be on our way.

Once outside we walked silently for a time as the crowds of tourists and natives shuffled past. Tanemghurt in her robes and veil and I in a long skirt and flowing blouse; we fit well amid the throng hurrying home before dark. The bandages extending down my arms and across the tops of my hands drew occasional looks but Fadil was walking close and turning to look at us. This would indicate that we were together and therefore untouchable. Finally, I could be quiet no longer and I turned to Tanemghurt, causing Fadil to stop also.

"Look," I began, "I understand your concern here but are we doing this the best way? We don't know who the person was or where they even came from, we're just guessing at this point."

"Yes," said Tanemghurt her luminous, impassioned eyes peeking out behind her veil, "but it is a lead, a thin piece of information that may bring us to an answer. All we can do is to continue asking."

Fadil stepped closer and began to speak to his sister in their native tongue. She turned to me and translated, "My brother too is concerned that we go on this goose chase. Please, Ms Devon, I have no right to ask you but I am driven by my own heart to take you on this journey with me. Perhaps you think us foolish or simply curious children trying to solve a riddle, but it is more than that. It is a need to secure my belief in what I know is true. The miracles cannot have been a hoax." Her demeanor began to change as if she were aging before my eyes. "Doctor Livingston, I am a college woman. I have been trained in the medical field and what I have seen I know without pretense or fantasy. I have seen the people healed with prayer. It is real and I must do my best to look into the eyes of the one I saw as being responsible for this. We have believed this was a Catholic priest but my eyes tell me that is not the person who spoke so knowingly with us in the cave. I am not curious, Doctor Livingston, I am driven."

"Okay," I sighed, "I have some time available and my own curiosity is getting the better of me. I suppose this will be the best way to proceed."

Tanemghurt threw her arms around my shoulders as if she had returned to her more youthful persona. "You will not regret your kindness, my friend."

"I hope not" I whispered as I returned her hug. I looked at Fadil and noticed him slowly shaking his head as he nervously watched the passing crowds. He turned toward the street and managed to hail a passing taxi. We were in front of my hotel and now safe passage for their journey home was assured.

We met again the next morning in the library at the University which contained a few more books as well as a Christian bible in the reference section and access to the internet. We were aware that we might be less conspicuous here, along with the possibility of a slightly less biased data base. Their hours of operation were longer and my credentials as an American professor gave us some extra perks not available to the average student. Although still under the eye of Islam the school was able to offer a little more rounded view of the outside world along with some of the worldwide web. Tanemghurt now dressed in a headscarf that allowed me to see her face.

This time I began to ask some of the basic questions I had been harboring that had very little to do with the Ancient One. How did the Catholic Church actually operate? What was the basis for their beliefs? Tanemghurt and Fadil were eager to show me books and websites that they thought might answer some of the questions. The books were old and tucked away in places less obvious to the general public and some of the websites were restricted but there was information available for the curious mind.

The organization of the group is a hierarchy with a leader elected by a select group of members of the church. The system is actually set up along lines that seem almost military in some ways. There is a person who is called a pope and a large majority of people who call themselves Catholic recognize him as the earthly head of the church. It is a worldwide community made up of ordained men, vowed men and women and the rest of the folks referred to as the laity. They tend to hold a belief that they are the continuation of the Christian community founded by Jesus Christ before he returned to heaven, something they call apostolic succession. It was all interesting in an historical sense and went back over two thousand years. Much of what I read there seemed to deal with countries on the European continent but I knew from my own grasp of history that the North of Africa was a place which once seethed with Christian activity.

The monastery at Beni Abbes, according to a tourists guide book of Algeria, was operated by a group called the Little Brothers of the Gospel, a fraternity created by Charles de Foucauld, a Frenchman who came to Algeria in the early 1900's. This was well over 100 years ago and could have fallen into the time span alluded to in the story of Azerwal but it certainly did not stretch back to a time before the religion of Islam existed. In no book, furthermore, was there a mention of miracles or healing among the members of the Little Brothers.

After eight straight hours of reading and flipping through histories I grew a bit exasperated.

"Tanemghurt," I said "I don't think this is really getting us any closer to finding your Ancient One. The history and teachings are all fine but how does this relate to the person we are searching for? The stories you were told by Azerwal would make this monk or whatever over a thousand years old, the monastery at Beni Abbes doesn't even appear to go back that far?"

"Well, I don't know." The frustration showed in her voice also. "Somehow, we thought there had to be stories or, I don't know, something about a great healer who came to the desert or passed through the villages. Why would the stories of my people, who are a small minority in this great world, be so much richer than the stories of the other peoples?"

"Good question." I answered. I didn't want what she believed, to be a fantasy. I wanted what I knew I felt in that dark cave to be the real truth, a truth that could not be taken away by the light of day. I looked at my little friend and realized that she was near tears. We agreed to wrap things up for this day but to meet again in the morning.

Upon returning to the hotel there was a message from the university. I was cleared for a three month leave by the board of regents. They had thoughtfully included a get-well card in the envelope. There was also a note from Janine reminding me that Ramadan was fast approaching and hoping that I would be careful. I had not even thought of much beyond my own needs and concerns. I began considering the possibility that I would continue my search from another country.

The next morning, Tanemghurt and Fadil had me meet them at the Catholic Church in Rabat, the Saint Pierre Cathedral. There I witnessed a ritual that left me with more questions than answers. The service was in Arabic so I understood few if any of the words; but the thing that I remembered was Tanemghurt's statement that all such services were essentially the same throughout the world. She said they were usually in the language native to that country but the order and words spoken during the Mass were always the same. The people showed great reverence for what was happening at the table in the front of the church. The minister spoke before the crowd but only for a few minutes and there was no great harangue that I might have associated with a call to repent. Later Tanemghurt told me that the priest had explained the meaning of the passage read from the Catholic Bible and compared it to everyday life in Rabat. I thought it interesting that these people would create a religious mystique around the ordinary lives of human beings.

Following the service, I went with Fadil and Tanemghurt to the home of their relatives; they were very proud to show off their friend from the United States to their cousins. It was there that I learned even more about the family. Tanemghurt was the eldest child of a wealthy merchant who had lived and worked in Adrar, Algeria. The family is Amazigh or Berber to the Western culture. They are all Roman Catholic and work very hard to maintain their religious identity in spite of living in an Islamic country. As the oldest child, Tanemghurt was given her name, which is Amazigh for tall one, in defiance of the Arab rules to give up their native ways. The two younger brothers were given Islamic names in order to allow them to fit in and be a part of the community where they would live. Their father adored Tanemghurt and ordered that she be called by an Arabic name, Nabihah, when in public, in order to protect her. He wished to give her the best that life could offer so, when she was old enough, she was sent away to the United States for school with the idea that she would become a doctor, perhaps marry a wealthy man and eventually bring them all to America. Tanemghurt had other ideas and when her father died as an innocent bystander in a conflict in the market square, she returned home and reclaimed her given name.

Their mother was a receptionist for the university in Adrar. She also carried both an Amazigh and an Arabic name which she used when necessary. She was a convert to Catholicism but continued in the faith even after her husband was killed. The Amazigh people are a close-knit group and maintain family ties far beyond what I have experienced in my own family. They begged me to stay with them but I returned to the hotel to ponder all the things I had learned and try to put them in perspective. Tanemghurt and Fadil agreed to meet me the next day at another Catholic Church close to their cousin's home where another priest had agreed to talk with us.

I cannot say it was a restful evening but the time alone gave me a chance to consider all the things I had seen up to that night. Morocco was beautiful. It is an ancient country filled with sights and sounds that are at once mysterious and yet vaguely familiar, an area that has drawn people from many different parts of the world for centuries. From my hotel balcony I watched a spectacular sunset and listened as the Imam called for evening prayer. The dust of the desert hung in the air as the sound of car horns blended with the cry of camels near the cities edge.

Although Islam is the dominant religion of the region, people of other faiths are allowed to live there especially if they come, as many do, from Europe. These are mostly expatriates from Spain or France who have chosen to remain in Morocco rather than return home. They come and stay and raise their families here. Those children may often go on to build lives and raise families even though they may look and act more like their European cousins. What a mixture of life. We scientists are always so busy categorizing and dividing people and things into separate lists; in North Africa it is as if the people are all jumbled together. I was reminded of my home in the United States and how so many had come from so many different places to create an idealized culture where all philosophies could be part of the community. It's not easy. America, for all its' "melting pot" reputation, still fights bigotry and separation issues. There, in Morocco things are not as ideal and devastating wars large and small are fought over philosophies.

I once again remembered the sing song of the words I had heard across the blackness of the cave. "Christ is a light we must search for…"and "to each heart a perfect answer, perfect to that one alone…" It must be the rhythm of the sounds that made it so hypnotic; although there was also the reality that millions of people seem to find some relief from the stresses of their lives when they are able to cling to these beliefs. I ducked back into my room from the small balcony. Staring into the dressing table mirror I forced my mind back into its logical place. "Yes," I told myself aloud. "History has been filled for centuries with groups of persons professing a belief centered on this figure. The total truth of this belief system is that we cannot, in this century, know for certain that such a human being existed; but it is quite true that philosophies proposed in his name have had a profound effect on the ability of civilizations to coexist on this planet. Although not all persons have followed a path of peacefulness, it would appear that many of the teachings proffered in his school of thought have been beneficial." There it was, my memorized tidbit of teaching that kept me out of trouble in the classroom; non committal, hopefully inoffensive and neutral in bias. I reached for a paperback novel and lay back on the bed to read myself to sleep.

CHAPTER 7
A CONSIDERATION

Devon had stopped her story and was looking at a point above my head. I turned to see the restaurant manager was standing behind me with a quiet smile.

"I'm so sorry to interrupt but the storm is over" he walked around to the side of our table almost bowing as he came. "We still have no electricity so the owner has advised us all to lock up and leave."

"Oh certainly," I answered reaching for my wallet.

He raised his hand, "Please, Dr. Hanesworthy, we have been given permission to give you this one on the house, besides the cash register won't work without electricity."

I suddenly realized the young man was one of my former students. His name did not leap to mind but I did manage to remember his face. Devon was already standing beside him.

"Hi, Jimmy," she offered a hug. "How are you?"

The manager shuffled and blushed but did not reach for her embrace. "Oh, okay, Dr Livingston, it's good to see you again."

"You take care, now." Devon reached for his limp hand and shook it.

I threw a group of small bills on the table knowing that the meal may have been free but the service was not. We proceeded to the door with the help of the manager's flashlight. The storm had ended so we were able to walk to the parking lot without getting more than our shoes wet. The night air was chilly and the only light was the occasional far away burst of lightning in the eastern sky. We huddled close and moved rapidly along the walk to the side of the building where our cars were parked next to each other.

"You are good friends with the manager?" I finally said.

"Oh, yes," Devon answered through chattering teeth, "We were in a few classes together and then we did some field projects not too long ago. Nice guy, maybe we were sort of close for a little while. He's probably married or something."

"Listen," I said as she opened her car door, "Would you like to go somewhere else and talk, I sense that your story isn't finished?"

"I don't think so," she smiled weakly as she slid into the driver's seat. "I need to get home, it's late, and I have early appointments, but thanks for dinner."

I held the door open an extra moment watching her reaction in the light from the car's interior. "Would it be alright if I called you? Maybe to-morrow after I get out of class?"

Devon hesitated slightly, and then smiled warmly. "Okay, but how about if we meet again on Friday? I really need the rest of the week to get some things done. Can we meet in the lounge on Friday?"

She flashed her eyes at me and I knew I would be there. "Sure, I think I can be there about the same time as today."

"Great" she grinned. "See you then."

She shut the door and started the engine. I stood there in the black parking lot waving at the rain-stained window. Surely, she would be there at the hour she mentioned. I turned to my own vehicle and fished for the keys in my pocket. Nothing even remotely key like slid between my fingers. Lightning flashed somewhere off in the distance and I saw the sparkle of something metallic on my car seat.

"Oh God," I moaned, in all the rush with putting up the top I had locked my keys in my car once again. Suddenly lights all around me came on. Three figures came around the corner of the building at that same moment.

"Oh, no" a woman's voice spoke "does this mean we have to go back in and work."

"Nope" a male voice answered "I don't think these lights will stay on. I think the power company will take them all back off line in a minute and we'll still be in the dark."

The third voice said, "Even if they stay on, I'm going home. No one else is going to come out tonight."

"Hi, Doc" the woman's voice called. "You, okay?" It was the last waitress we had encountered. Her car was located next to mine.

"Actually, no" I stammered "I seem to have locked my keys inside."

"Aww" she drawled, "Don't we all do that sometimes. You just wait here a minute and let me see if I have something we can use to get that door popped open."

She leaned into her vehicle and pulled out an article of clothing lying in the backseat. She deftly pulled it loose exposing a wire hanger. She tossed the cloth back into the dark recesses of the car and then proceeded to bend and articulate the wire for another use. As she moved toward my car, I began to have visions of this woman shredding the finish of my fine automobile in an attempt to rescue me. Suddenly the lights on the side of the building went out and we were plunged once again into darkness.

"Shit" the voice of the waitress exploded softly. "I bet Jim just turned everything off. Well, Doc, his pickup is just on the other side of mine. If you don't mind waiting around for a few he'll be out and maybe he can help you." She shoved her instrument of torture into my hand and returned to her car. "Y'all come back now." With a wave she slipped into her vehicle and was gone into the night.

I stood there holding the wire from the coat hanger like a dagger trying desperately to decide what I could do at this moment. I was locked out of my car. It was very nearly midnight. Although the lights on the building had gone out several large overhead lamps and the street lights stayed on allowing me enough illumination to see what had to be done. I had no roadside assistance policy and after a couple of experiences with calling all night locksmiths, I was not sure I wanted to spend that kind of money. As I truly had no idea how to use the weapon the waitress had handed me; I was without several resources.

Just then I heard the sound of footsteps and saw a familiar figure round the corner of the restaurant. It was indeed Jim, the manager and my heart leapt with anticipation that he might have the necessary knowledge to free me without much fanfare.

"Jim." I called in a friendly tone. "Is that you, then?"

"Hi Doctor Hanesworthy" he answered "everything okay?"

"Well, no actually" I felt embarrassed again and began to stammer. "I seem to have locked my keys in here and the waitress tried to help but I don't really know how to make this work."

"Oh sure" Jim stepped next to me and took the wire from my hand. "Let me just get in here if you will. I have to do this all the time for my employees. Sometimes I think they should put that on the application for manager. You know, can applicant open car doors with a coat hanger." He chuckled at his own joke and began to insert the wire between the window and the door. I cringed and looked away. "It just takes a little time. Hmm"

"Hmm," I questioned. "Is that bad?"

"Oh no" he assured me "no problem, Doctor Hanesworthy. Some of them just take a little longer than others; we'll have you out of here in a jiffy."

Just then a police car rolled slowly by shining a spotlight into the parking area; Jim's head popped up and a small gasp escaped his lips. The patrol car braked and backed slightly before turning to enter the area where we stood. I knew it looked suspicious, but was certain I could put things to rights with the officer. The window on the passenger side slid down about half way as the vehicle neared us and a voice called from inside.

"Is everything okay, gentlemen?"

"Yes, officer" I bent to peer at the voice. "My keys are locked…"

"Doctor Hanesworthy" the voice exploded and the driver's side door opened. "I didn't see it was you." A young man in uniform exited the car and came around to us. "Hey, Jim, you need some help."

Jim's hand slid past me to greet the officer and I backed away. "Craig, how are you, man."

"Good, good" the officer was tall and blond and about the same age as the manager. Again, a face I recognized without the name.

"You're closing a little early, Jim?" the officer asked. Jim nodded. "Yeah, the storm got a lot of things on this block but the worst was the fire at Donnell's Pub, burned it right down to the ground. Don and Belva weren't the only ones in there so we were lucky everyone got out safe."

"We heard the sirens," Jim added. "We just sort of laid low in here."

Both men were turned away from me as they began to work on the car in earnest. I pondered the number of individuals who must live in this town who may have attended one of my classes. It suddenly seemed so awful and insensitive of me not to know each one by name. But how could I possibly do that? Ten years of classes of students, some as large as 350 bodies all stuffed into folding seats or lined up on benches. In any given year I might teach ten or twelve classes; occasionally, in the last few years there would be three or four different groups using the same books and subject. How could I keep all those beings in mind especially once the classes were finished? So why had Devon been able to know our friend Jim? She'd nearly leapt at him there at the table. My focus changed from my own thoughts to the quiet conversation of my rescuers.

Craig began, "So what was the professor doing here tonight? I thought he was a real hermit?"

"Believe it or not, I think he was on a date" Jim answered. "You'll never guess who."

"Oh yeah, who" Craig questioned?

"Doctor Devon Livingston" Jim stated emphasizing each word.

"No" Craig said incredulously "I thought she was in Europe or something."

"Well, she was definitely here tonight." Jim said. "She tried to give me one of her big old friendly hugs but didn't…"
I cleared my throat as if to remind them that I was there. I had really heard quite enough. Suddenly Jim pulled back and the door of the car did indeed pop open.

Craig turned to me, "Well, got you on the road again, Professor. Have a good night."
"Yes, thank you" I tried to smile but I'm not sure it came across. The officer moved quickly to his patrol car and backed out into the street. I turned my attention to Jim.

"Truly, Jim" I stammered "thank you. I don't know how to do those things and I appreciate your rescuing me."

My friend wore a slightly sheepish look as if he were unsure how much I had overheard. "It's no big deal, Doctor Hanesworthy. Like I said I do this a lot." He handed me the twisted wire then seemed to think better of that and tossed into the back of an old pickup truck, the only other vehicle in the lot.

"Please" I said unable to think of anything else to say "call me Fred. We're now good friends and I won't forget you." I extended my hand and Jim shook it.

"Okay, Fred" he said "you have a good night or should I say morning; seeing as how it's after midnight." He turned to go.

"Jim" my curiosity suddenly got the better of me. "Not meaning to be boorish but you did seem to know my dinner companion rather well. Were you classmates or something?"

He stopped and turned seeming to contemplate the question. "Well, yes…ah…maybe a little more than that." His speech pattern began to speed up as he attempted to explain. "I… ah…I don't want this to reflect on anything but…ah…we…that is…Devon and I…well, we had this relationship. Not that we still do, oh no, it was over years ago, long before she started teaching. It's…ah… well, you know how it is in college and you're young and you do dumb things and well. I'm not answering you very well, am I?"

"Actually, Jim" I leaned against my car as I spoke "you answered quite well. The past is the past and I'm really not fishing for anything, just a bit curious. You have a good rest of the night yourself." I smiled, grabbed the keys from the seat and sat down. It really didn't matter that Devon had been with other men. We were not that far along in our relationship. One could not technically have called this a date. The engine started and I headed for my apartment and a night of pondering.

Devon was lovely but she had always kept her distance, at least from me. She did seem capable of flirting with men, perhaps that was what he was referring to, and she might have been admitting to knowing him on a romantic level. Well, I have been in love or something like it with a woman, even married one. I hardly expected Devon to be virginal at this stage of her life. Driving through the deserted, rain-soaked streets was cleansing. I rolled my windows down and allowed the cool night air to envelope me. I started to put the top down but decided the rain might not be over with.

The next three days hummed along as usual lulling me back into the day-to-day rhythm of my ordinary life. I thought about Devon from time to time but what stuck out even more was the story she had been telling. I could not know if it was a conversion story but the first part, especially the time in the cave, made it sound like that. Religious conversion is a tricky thing.

My childhood was spent in the shadow of parents who fostered no particular religious preference and encouraged my siblings and me to follow our own path. I was always torn between the theory of freedom and the lack of knowledge this created. Yes, we were free but we never really knew what we were free from. I had one very close friend in grammar school whose parents continually asked me to accompany them to church services. Brad was an only child and very spoiled so he was in the habit of always having his own way in things. One way they had of getting him to attend with them was by inviting a friend to spend the weekend. I found it interesting simply because there was nothing like it in my own home. There were other children present at the church and if Brad became boring, I could always play with one of the other boys. Memories of bible stories and Jesus being my loving friend were all quite nice and helped me feel less estranged once I began studying in earnest to achieve my goals in anthropology. One cannot go through school in middle -America without hearing about the Judeo-Christian belief systems. One may not be willing to pursue in earnest the teachings of one congregation over another, but the general knowledge is always there and the history is a great part of Western Civilization. Still, this is not conversion.

I remembered the bit Devon shared about her conversation in the hotel room, the politically correct statement that identifies the Christian philosophy as existing without making a statement either pro or con. We were all educated that way. This is a state-run system of higher learning and we are all coached to steer that middle ground that admits to no affiliation. Her change of heart was foreseeable. She had been brought near physical death and then rescued. The psychological reaction to that has been told a thousand times.

Devon was interesting, her search was compelling, but it was still simple religious conversion. She would probably tell me how she had come to find 'the Lord'. I had heard it a hundred times from students and a few faculty. It usually came in the spring in connection with the Easter season. Some individuals could become very intense in their determination that they had been 'saved'. Some part of me always wondered from what they had actually been saved, but nevertheless; I did not care to be witness to this business. By Friday I had determined that I would meet with her and find a way to say we could be colleagues but nothing more. In that manner when her story became trite and boring, not listening was an honest option.

I questioned a couple of my associates concerning the return of Dr. Livingston and inevitably seemed to receive a snide comment or two about her apparent lack of virtue. The most direct came from my office mate, Dr. Smith. He questioned whether I, as a free and available bachelor, was planning on spending some personal time with her. I offered that I was considering so and he cautioned that she did not seem to be the type of woman who could choose just one partner. It was a rather nice way of saying she was not a 'nice' girl. Still the story she shared was not about promiscuity or virtue but about something else, or so I thought.

I bound up the stairs on Friday afternoon as planned, rounded the corner into the room only to find it filled with half a dozen teaching associates lounging about and talking in clumps of twos and threes. This is how it normally was rather than the empty room I had found on Tuesday last. The person I had come to meet did not appear but the gathering would allow me to mingle quietly while I waited. Among those present was Janine, the geologist who had so tested Devon's patience.

"Doctor Longley" I hailed "how are you?"

"Well, Doctor Hanesworthy," she beamed "I'm fine and you?"

"Quite well" I answered "thank you. Are your classes going well?"

"Yes" she nearly giggled. This was an odd reaction. "Summer is nearly upon us." She was looking at me as if some delicious secrets were hiding between us. We were then joined by Frank Jefferson and the Andersens all smiling and staring at me. Joseph Smith, my office mate came gliding next to me and placed a bottled soft drink in my hand. He also shared the same secretive smile. I acknowledge that I am, by and large, a quiet person given to speaking mostly when spoken to and that of late I had become more verbose. Perhaps, they had noted this and were curious.

"Well, Fred" Joseph trumpeted pounding me on the back as he spoke "how are you these days?"

"As well as I was this morning, I suppose." I knew we had spoken briefly as we passed in the hallway entering and exiting our combined office space. What, I wondered, had changed?

Frank spoke up "You been pretty busy lately, Fred?" The group seemed to snicker.

"Just the usual" I suddenly felt very odd and exposed. The overheard conversation about my being a hermit suddenly came to mind. What on earth are these people thinking? Unexpectedly the mood shifted and the attention of the entire room seemed drawn to a spot behind me. Smiles increased and nods were given. I turned to see Devon entering the room. Her clothing was casual but very becoming. The crowd drifted away as each person began to offer an excuse for leaving the room.

"Hello, Devon" I said evenly

"Fred" she returned the tone "how are you?"

"Good" I was suddenly aware that only Frank seemed to be hanging about, abruptly Janine stuck her head back in the doorway

"Frank" she barked "get out here now."

Frank, as always, did as ordered. As soon as he exited, both Devon and I burst into laughter easing the tension which had been built up by the awkwardness of the situation.

"Can you possibly tell me what that was all about?" I asked.

"Well," Devon began "let me guess. You got here a few minutes ahead of me and found yourself totally surrounded by various friends, all of them smiling like the cat that caught the canary." I nodded. "You, of course, have absolutely no idea what is going on." Again, I nodded. She shook her head.

"Fred" she took my arm and walked me to the couch. "You have become the subject of happy gossip. We, that is, you and I, have somehow become the topic of the day on campus. Our dinner and discussion has turned into a date and there are a few of our friends who would like to make us a couple." A deep sigh escaped me as I folded on to the couch. "I can't tell you why people are like this but I know they are. I'm the same way with my friends, I want them to feel good and so I place my good feelings on them and it all becomes so…I don't know…silly."

"You would think we were still in college." I managed to say.

"Fred," the sparkling blue eyes stared into mine. "We are still in college. I can't say that this is a problem but let's face it, we live a certain lifestyle that fosters a way of thinking. The question may be what can we do about it?"

"How about if we do nothing, since this is not our situation but rather someone else's speculation concerning our actions?" I offered.

"That sounds appropriate to me." Devon responded. "Can we start our meeting or date or whatever we started out to have tonight?"

"Of course, so, how have you been?" I settled in and turned my attention to my companion. "I trust you had a good week?"

Devon relaxed, "I certainly did. I have taken a position here at the university and will start teaching again in the fall. I also have some friends arriving from Algeria. They were in need of housing so I have been able to get that situation all in order. I would say that things are coming along very well."

"Oh, really" I said "your little guide friend?"

"Yes," she said "and her brother Fadil. He starts in the A&S College and Tanemghurt will continue her medical studies."

"Their family won't mind?" I questioned.

Devon seemed to freeze momentarily then lowered her head. "I don't think so," her eyes seemed to glisten with tears as she raised her gaze to mine, "I'm afraid they have lost many of their relatives in the fighting again. Not their mother, thank God, or little brother but some cousins."

"Well, that's awful," I said, "I don't have to know them to feel a bit of sorrow with that news"

"I would have wished it to be any other way," Devon shook her head but then seemed to brighten a bit. "They were such a happy family. Some people I got to know and care about. The time spent with them will remain in my memories for the rest of my days."

"I'm intrigued again" I said "can you continue?" I had promised myself that I would at least listen.

Her eyes began to shift as the memories floated in. "Well, let's see, we were in Rabat, Morocco near the end of summer. Ramadan was approaching and I was scheduled to meet Tanemghurt at my hotel for another foray into the search for the Ancient One.

CHAPTER 8
MEETINGS

This time Tanemghurt arrived at my hotel alone. She explained that Fadil was needed to take care of some other business for the family and they felt we would be alright without him since we were going to be in a part of the city familiar to them. We prepared to take a taxi from the hotel, which attracted a lot less attention. I looked every bit the part of a tourist wandering the streets with my guide; in suitable dress, a long multi-colored skirt and one of my tan safari shirts. My friend helped me find an appropriately hued scarf to cover my hair and we were off. The morning was cool and clear with a promise of the sweltering afternoon heat not far behind.

The man we met was Fr. Christian Amad-Benoit at the Church of Saint Fancois d'Assise. We had not arrived in time for services but a member of Tanemghurt's family had been there and set an appointment for us to meet. He led us to a large library in the home where he lived. It was a huge room with books running from floor to ceiling. One massive library table dominated the center with huge heavy chairs arranged about its' perimeter. I estimated that the room contained nearly a thousand volumes in French, English, as well as Arabic; all concerning, I supposed, the teachings of the Catholic Church. Fr. Christian was a heavy set, jovial man who was only too happy to share his knowledge and his books with the little American doctor. He also listened to Tanemghurt's tale of the healing monk and like his fellow priest, recalled no personal knowledge of any such person. At least this time she was not scolded for her questions. I reminded myself to remain calm if such a confrontation were to ensue but fortunately for all, there was only concern and smiles.

"I am so sorry, my dears," he spoke in French- accented English "I have never heard of your great healing person. I have some histories here that might mention it, they concern the local church." He drew down two dusty volumes and blew across the tops to dislodge the particles. "Did you know, for instance that the great and wondrous saint by the name of Augustine of Hippo was a Berber who was born in the city now known as Souk Ahras in Algeria." He looked directly at Tanemghurt as he spoke.

Tanemghurt displayed great joy although I knew we had been looking at a history which contained this information, just days before.

"I have heard this name, Father Christian" she seemed to bubble like a young child. The priest chuckled indulgently as he bent across the table gently placing the book before her and began to turn the pages for her. He smiled above her, murmuring as if he were speaking to a five-year-old showing her pictures and drawings. He seemed oblivious to the reality that he was dealing with a well-educated, multi-lingual young woman. She seemed just as willing to go along with the game. It was a prejudicial display and it made my skin crawl.

Suddenly, he clapped his hands together and stood erect. "Well, my dear ones, I must go out now. My housekeeper is here if you need anything." At that moment a slender, elderly woman dressed in long skirt and kerchief, appeared at the door of the office carrying a small hat which she handed to the reverend. Shooting a look at us which said 'you better not be touching anything'; she turned and followed her employer back down the hall.

Tanemghurt and I found ourselves left alone with the mass of books and what seemed to be the balance of a day to find information. A look of frustration flooded her face as she turned and whispered "I thought surely, he would tell us something. Why do they not know?" All I could do was shrug as the question drilled through my brain, "Why are you asking me, I'm the outsider here?"

I placed my eyes on another book in front of me and tried to find a place to begin reading until I heard the door close at the front of the house. Then I turned to my friend

"Tanemghurt," I whispered "why did you go along with that? Don't you think he treated you like a child?'

She cocked her head to one side. "But Ms Devon, I must always show respect. He is after all the priest." With the last word her eyes were cast down in reverence. It was not the only lesson I would learn about the attitude called for in dealing with this culture and this religion. A lot of what occurs between men and women in this country is about inequality. Men have power and even good men like Fadil, simply have all the control. For us in Western culture this just seems wrong but it is the way they live and it does bear on their way of being religious.

We sat in silence then, pouring over the volumes before us until we heard the noon cry of the Imam calling the faithful to prayer. The little housekeeper suddenly whisked into the room carrying a tray with small sandwiches and drinks. We thanked her profusely as she grimaced and rolled her eyes. Surely, we were not that menacing, perhaps it was just a disruption to her routine that felt so bothersome. As we finished our meal, Tanemghurt excused herself to find the restroom. When she returned, I asked directions from her and took a turn myself. Down the hall stood the housekeeper, peering intently at me, as if she was checking to see that we were not stealing the towels.

When I returned to the library, Tanemghurt was gone again. I peeked out the door but saw only the dark hallway. I knew I was in the proper room because the books lay open to the pages we had turned to before I took my leave. The trays with our lunch items had been cleared away which was unsettling but I decided to continue on until someone showed up. If nothing else I still had my cell phone and several phone numbers for my guides. If they had done something to her, I could call for help.

A book caught my attention, lying open on the table at Tanemghurt's place. It told a story concerning the works of Augustine, an ancient bishop of Hippo and the man Fr. Christian had pointed out to Tanemghurt. He had been a very wise man who had an immense impact on the Catholic Church in those beginning years a century or more after the original apostles had all died. He was a philosopher and theologian who spent his own early days as a pagan intellectual but eventually joined his Berber mother in her Christian faith. He became a bishop in Numidia (Algeria) and wrote extensively about salvation, grace, and sin. An Algerian Berber being leader of the Church; given the prejudice I had witnessed in the hospital and even here, I was incensed. Tanemghurt's observation that the history of her people was rich and filled with beauty was true. Prejudice and jealousy work to destroy that beauty.

Another book lay next to it open to a second great person, Thomas of Aquinas. He was born many centuries later in Italy, but still was talked about in a manner that showed his immense impact on the teachings of the Church. These were men who had a direct influence on the direction and philosophies of the Catholic Church in its' early years. I wondered what made their words more important than others. I had seen both names in other history books and listened to synoptic statements about them in various classes in college, but now I was attaching the names to a very specific time and place. The words floated into my head again "if you seek Him, He will find you." I stopped musing at the sound of voices in the hall.

Tanemghurt returned to the room with an odd look on her face. The housekeeper followed her in as if she were shooing an errant child back into place. My friend sat, shook her head and leaned close to me "I can't get past the bathroom without the housekeeper coming after me," she whispered.

"Where else did you need to go?" I questioned.

"Well, I wanted to check on my brother." She explained, "Ramadan starts tonight and I want to make sure we have a safe way home."

I reached for my cell phone and held it out to her.

Suddenly, behind the housekeeper, loomed the figure of Fr. Christian. He had returned from his appointment and was now ready to rejoin our party. Tanemghurt rose from her seat and curtsied. I was not as quick and so remained seated as the old priest took a chair opposite us at the library table. He smiled and appeared not to notice that I had not bowed to him but the housekeeper was obviously incensed as she scurried out of the room.

"So how are we now, my dears," he intoned through his graying beard. "Have we found the answer to our long sought after questions?"

"Actually," I answered "we haven't found the identity of our healing monk but we certainly have found lots of interesting facts. As Tanemghurt mentioned I am not Catholic so a lot of this is new information for me."

"Ah, but my friend is very wise, Fr Christian" Tanemghurt interjected as if to protect me from any offense that my position as an outsider might incur.

"Good" he wrinkled his brow at me. "Tell me, Ms. Doctor, what is the purpose of your search? Do you look to be healed of your wounds?" He glanced to my arms where bandages clearly showed beneath the sleeves.

"Well," I tried to consider just how much to tell him about myself. "I don't think I need any medical healing. The hospital here has been very capable of taking care of my physical problems. I believe I'm just trying to help Tanemghurt find the person she is seeking."

"Why?" his eyes stared in to mine and I flinched at the point-blank question and the changing tone in his voice. "You are an American, you can walk away from this place tomorrow and no one will consider it odd. Why are you choosing to stay?" His tone was no longer so happy.

I felt caught like a rat in a maze. I had been considering what it all meant but had not come to a full answer for myself. Perhaps his questions were just echoes of my own heart. In the telling of the story, Tanemghurt had hit the high points. Like any good reporter she told the when, where, and what but left out the penetrating conversations we had shared in the darkness of the cave. How could I tell this stranger that the simple sing song rhymes of a voice in the night were worming their way into my heart? How do I relate to anyone the feelings that make no sense to me?

Finally, I found a voice. "I am not sure how to answer your questions. Believe me, I have asked myself the same thing." I glanced at Tanemghurt who was studying my face. "I know that part of it is because Tanemghurt asked me to help but the other part is my own curiosity. I never thought of myself as a religious person. Oh, I've been to churches in the US but not any Catholic ones. I sort of accept that there may be an intelligence behind all that occurs on the earth. One can hardly go through grad school without being confronted with the questions. I've just never been personally involved before."

Tanemghurt rose and excused herself. Perhaps she was going to try calling her brother or perhaps our questions and statements had become more than she felt comfortable with. I had seen no indication from the priest that she should be sent from the room but I suddenly felt relieved when she walked out.

Fr. Christian stroked his beard. "So, you are on a quest for your own heart as well. Do you seek a church or a God?"

I blinked at the question. I had never considered that there was a difference and yet it was, at that moment, abundantly clear that this was the truth. "I... I don't believe I know the answer to that yet."

His face softened as he shuffled in his chair. "Let me try to explain, for I see in you a person who comes new and fresh to the fountain of light. I am a priest of the Roman Catholic Church and so anything I tell you will be colored by my own belief. It is not easy but I shall try to explain for you in a nutshell." It seemed like a fair and honest assessment of reality. He could hardly be preparing to teach me about Islam even though we were in a country immersed in that teaching.

"You admit by your own statement," he began, "that there possibly exists an intelligence which controls the world as we know it. It is the belief of millions of persons that this is true and that we learned of this truth most recently through the teachings of a man Jesus the Christ. This man was born over two thousand years ago and we believe that we have created a society which attempts to follow His teachings in order to grow closer to that being that we have named God. We believe that Jesus Christ was and is the living son of that God creator and we live with the blessings of the Trinity. The Trinity takes in the Father, the Son and The Holy Spirit, whom Jesus promised to us at the time of his resurrection into heaven. The society we have created is the

Catholic Church which you see in all its glory today. The knowledge we have is based on the deposit of Faith contained in the Holy Bible and our Sacred Traditions." He paused.

Somehow this did not equate to what I felt or what I had heard so many weeks before in the cavernous darkness. It was simple and concrete but lacked something. I looked at my hands and tried to put it all in perspective.

"Well," he breathed, "perhaps the nutshell version is a little too flat?"

I spoke now from my core. "It's a good explanation but it doesn't exactly fit with some things the woman in the cave told me." I looked up as Fr. Christian cocked his head to listen more closely. "The woman, the Ancient One as they called her, she spoke of finding this Jesus. She said that one had to seek him out and that if one was successful there would be healing of wounds and not just physical ones but wounds of the heart. I also listened to Tanemghurt tell me about people in her village being changed by what they came to know after visiting with the person in the cave. They both made it sound like your Church can offer these things and that everyone in the world might be able to have this healing."

"How beautiful that is" the priest mused "I would say that this is correct. Is it your heart that needs to heal? Do you seek a change within?"

This was another point-blank question that I had only just begun to ask myself.

"I've had a really normal life, some good stuff, some bad stuff. There are always parts I need to let go of but for the most part I've liked what I have created for myself." I tried to answer.

"Did you create or did God create? It is a very deep question, I think." The priest was no longer looking at me but at his own hands placed palms down, as if this was a question, he might ask himself.

Suddenly the quiet reflective room was rocked by a loud thud followed by a strong concussion behind me. Father Christian rose with arms outstretched as books began to rain down on me.

"Duck under the desk" He cried.

I dropped and crawled quickly forward as I heard the bookcase come crashing against the table above me. I looked up as the dust began to clear only to see Fr. Christian rolled into a large ball next to me, half in and half out of the cover of the massive library table.

"Father Christian" I spoke tentatively.

"Dear God," he said "what the hell was that?"

The priest, moving very quickly for a man his size, rolled up onto all fours.

"You are well, my dear?" he was breathless and terror filled his eyes.

"Yes" I quavered. "I'm just a little shaken up."

The feet of the housekeeper appeared at the door as Father Christian began to back out of the space. I wriggled around to follow him. The housekeeper was wailing in Arabic as she tried to move the books that had fallen across the table on to the carpet near her feet. He began to try and console her in her native tongue. As I cleared the desk another bookshelf wobbled and then toppled spilling its contents on the rest of the table. The housekeeper shrieked and covered her face with her hands. Father Christian placed his hands on her shoulders and pressed her into an empty chair. He produced a chain of beads from his pocket and placed them in her hands. She made a cross in front of her body and began to rock back and forth whispering in Arabic.

The priest headed for the door as Tanemghurt ran in still holding my cell phone to her ear. She squeezed past him and ran to hug me.

"Oh, Devon" she breathed "You are okay." She began to cry.

"I'm fine" I was actually shaking "I rolled under the table. What was that… a bomb?"

With that word Tanemghurt gave me a terrified look. Things were tough in Morocco but not usually that bad. Her attention was returned to the voice on the phone. She began to talk rapidly trying not to cry. She nodded several times and then hung up handing me the phone.

"That was my brother" she looked relieved "he comes for us now in my uncle's car."

I pushed her to the door past the rocking housekeeper and down the hall. In the entryway we found Father Christian holding a young man bleeding profusely from a head wound. Tanemghurt moved quickly to help the young man to sit on a bench near the open front door.

"It was a car" Father Christian stated "somehow this young man ran off the road and into the side wall of my home. There are towels in the kitchen, please?" He pointed me toward the next room and I ran in to find any form of cloth I could see. I'm not good at injured people, I tend to panic.

When I returned Tanemghurt was sitting next to the victim attempting to stop the bleeding with her hand. She immediately began to make a compress from the towels and had the boy apply pressure. She placed him down on the bench and put his feet level with his head. Obviously, she had received enough medical training to know what to do in an emergency.

Father Christian was on the telephone speaking quickly and emphatically in French. It seemed as though the start of Ramadan had dwindled the police force and the chance for a rapid response was remote. Again, there was a terrified shriek as the housekeeper entered the scene. She ran crying to the young man and attempted to wedge herself between Tanemghurt and the boy. Father Christian intervened and once again grabbed his servant and tried to comfort her.

"The boy is her nephew" Father explained "she is fearful. It appears to me that you have some medical training" he said to Tanemghurt. "Please proceed until the authorities arrive."

The priest continued to shush the woman as her screams turned to whimpers. I stood there feeling helpless with the cell phone in my hand. The thought ran through my mind "God, if you are there, please don't let this boy die. Let Tanemghurt's knowledge save his life." It wasn't much of a prayer but it was my first attempt. As an afterthought I added "and please, let them see the quiet dignity of this special young woman." If there is a God, shouldn't there be equality?

All of a sudden, Fadil came running up the walkway followed by the sound of sirens. Help was indeed on the way. Tanemghurt's brother assessed the situation and motioned for both of us to come with him. Tanemghurt shook her head and spoke to her brother indicating that she needed to stay with the patient until assistance arrived. He spoke to her in a whisper and they both looked at the housekeeper weeping into the arms of the priest.

"Go quickly" Fr. Christian said "I will take care of things here." He raised his hand and made a cross in the air. "May God bless you and keep you and make His face to shine upon you."

Both Tanemghurt and Fadil repeated the cross sign and bent one knee to the ground. I found myself making a bow. Somehow it seemed appropriate.

We scurried out and down the walk into the car waiting with the engine running. For the first time I saw the cause of my near demise. The church property sat at the end of another street forcing traffic to turn either right or left. Obviously, something had happened to prevent the driver from making that turn. An older model black sedan had run up the walk and right into the mud brick wall of the house. The hood was popped open and steam could be seen issuing from the damaged area. Neighbors were beginning to come out of their homes to inspect the accident.

Fadil pulled away from the curb before the authorities came into view. He continued along at a normal speed driving cautiously toward his family's home. Tanemghurt explained that on the evening of the first day of Ramadan, if a Christian is involved in an altercation they can be held until the end of the holy days, nearly a month, before they will have a chance to plead their case in court. We knew that Father Christian would explain for us but it was still best to be as far away as possible.

I sat back in the seat and wondered if things like that happened in America. The housekeeper had been incensed that my friend was touching her nephew even though it was clear to me that Tanemghurt knew better than anyone else in the room how to save his life. Scenes of race riots and peace marches and gay rights parades came immediately to mind. Prejudice is invasive and does not belong to one country or continent. These were Catholic people, the priest, the housekeeper, and Tanemghurt; how did prejudice enter in to that world?

We drove past their house and headed for the hotel. They would leave me there and then travel by car all the way back to Adrar. Tanemghurt was crying silently as we drove, all three of us in the large front seat. It felt as though it was the end but a small voice inside me was already saying it was a time to continue on. I held her hand and tried to assure her that I would not be far away. I wrote my cell number on a small sheet of paper and made her put it in her pocket.

CHAPTER 9
A PICNIC

We were back again in the same place. Devon and I sitting on a small couch in the old meeting room staring out at the campus below bathed in late spring shafts of waning sunlight. We were the same and yet, we were not. Now I looked at her and gazed purposefully into those bright blue eyes. The Devon I had known so casually before carried a shield against the world, now I could see beyond that barrier. There had always been a certain depth to her but now she was willing to let her heart show.

"This must be a stopping point" I said. "Do we head for the Dove again? They seem to know us there. Perhaps they would not be shocked at our spending time together at their tables. On the other hand, there may be less chance that something will fall and try to crush you if we stay here."

She smiled brightly "I brought a surprise. I hope you like it." She rose from the couch and opened a cabinet to one side of the picture window. Devon proceeded to withdraw a large wicker basket and a small sack. She placed the objects on a table before us and began to unload the basket. "It's just some sandwiches and a really cheap wine that I brought over earlier today. I thought, if we went to a place to eat there would be talk and the time might run out and …"

"This is great" I enthused. "I would never have thought of this."

I watched her carefully placing the items and knew that I was not going to tell her what I had come to say. She may be telling me a conversion story, she may be a woman of loose morals, she may even be trying to convert me to some belief system, but I no longer cared. She was delightful and at this moment I wished only to be delighted.

"Okay, Doctor Hanesworthy" she spoke as she sat back on the couch. "I have no idea if this is to your liking but it was something different." She picked up her filled wine glass and held it in salute waiting for me to lift mine also.

"To the story" I pronounced as we clicked rims.

"The story" she pronounced.

"Devon" I began, "have you thought about writing this all down and trying to sell it as a biographical tale or something?"

"Sure, I have." She spoke. "The thing is; I have wanted to tell someone the whole story for sometime just to hear what it sounds like. I know that may seem silly in some ways but I can't seem to just put it in writing. It's as if, this is a story lived, not written about."

"Well, I wouldn't call it silly but it is a bit odd." I offered. "Why not go on with this and then maybe I can help you decide."

She seemed satisfied with this and so continued on.

CHAPTER 10
A CHANGE IN PLANS

Fadil hurried to drop me at my hotel in Rabat before sunset. Tanemghurt continued to cry quietly as if in despairing acceptance. I assured her that we would continue to search but she would not be consoled. As they drove away, I wondered myself if I would ever see them again.

At the hotel I found a note waiting for me. I opened it as the elevator ascended. The note was from my mother and came with a money order in my name. It was not unusual for Mother to send me monetary amounts but it always seemed to accompany an appeal for something she thought I would not agree to. This time it was a request to meet her at a hotel in Paris in one week. The cash would more than cover the flight and reservations. There was no telling what she wanted. I toyed with the idea of calling to see if she would just tell me over the phone but I knew better. If Mother asked for my presence, nothing else would do. Since I have been an adult, she would allow me the freedom to say no but then she would not discuss her agendas if I declined the meeting. More than once I was shocked to find myself left alone without a word from her when she decided to move on and I had turned down her meeting.

I went to my room to ponder where I wanted to be next. I headed for the small balcony hoping for the same peace I had found there once before. My job was on hold. Although I was receiving no further monies from the university, my position would be waiting for me if I returned before the Christmas break. I enjoyed some of the work of teaching but often found I had little patience for the arrogant and spoiled children I encountered in the classroom. The research work I had been doing on pre-Columbian architecture in the Amazon basin had come to an end due to funding cuts. There was also the notion that I had seemingly escaped a chance at death for the second time in less than a year. That was something to ponder.

I had no love life. My last boyfriend and I had parted in an angry torrent of accusations of infidelity and mutual distrust, which was how most relationships ended for me unless they were really casual. I do not tend to one-night stands but I had not been totally opposed to them in my early twenties. Was that all there was to life? Working and finding that one great love with whom I might marry and settle into middle-class ennui?

I wasn't convinced that I could be part of a family or even love a child. I have friends who have them and make great claims about how they adore them and yet they treat them like objects. You see them running around in the beginning with little pink or blue bundles oohing and ahhing at each little movement. Then later it becomes, "Billy has to be at ball practice and I have a seminar, woe is me." "I'm so stressed, little Sally got an F in math, how can I deal with this?" I wonder if any of them knew that kids were such a hassle before they had them. They seem to see the kids as reflections of themselves.

On the other hand, there was the example of Tanemghurt's family. They had displayed such love for one another when I was with them. The good feelings even seemed to extend to me. Not just the offer of a meal but her brother's time in escorting us around and making sure we were safe. Much of what they presented told me that decisions never needed to be made alone. Always, there was some person to listen and help you decide the best course for your life.

She had shared in the cave that a part of her decision to leave college was based upon a comparison between the way her fellow students treated one another and the example of her family at home. Was this an affect of her tribal life or her Christian religion? I suspected it was a combination.

I did not see myself as a member of a tribe. No persons' life depended upon me to continue their existence. I began to see the life I had been living as selfish and unfulfilling. I had always kept so utterly busy whether learning or teaching, that there was no time to quietly reflect.

Perhaps that was the difference. The time in the cave had forced me to stop and look at who I am as well as how I lived my life. The challenge of the cave was to stay alive. There was no competition between the three of us. We had all wished and willed that all person's present would continue to survive. Perhaps I was just being sentimental because of the true physical danger we had endured.

I suddenly decided to try a very different decision. I grabbed my cell and called the house of Father Christian on the pretext of checking to see how his housekeeper and her nephew had fared through their ordeal. The phone rang for an extended period before the familiar voice answered in Arabic.

"Father Christian" I began. "This is Devon Livingston; I was at your home earlier this afternoon. I was just wondering how your housekeeper and her nephew were doing. Are they all, right?"

"Oh, of course, my dear," he responded in his French accented English, "they are both actually well considering the accident. The boy's wound was not as serious as it seemed. The head you know can bleed so very much. Mrs. Abidjan is actually fine, just very upset. How is your little friend?"

"You are referring to Tanemghurt?" I asked.

"Yes, she really did a good job in caring for young Ali." Father Christian still seemed surprised at her expertise.

"Truthfully" I answered wanting to sound flippant and angry, "Tanemghurt was a medical student in the United States a couple of years ago. She has had quite a bit of training. She is indeed, just fine."

"Ah" he seemed genuinely surprised, "I am afraid I often underestimate the capabilities of the Berber who live in this part of the world. In my native Europe, we sometimes see them as less than responsible citizens and that is not fair. I would ask you to forgive me for my sin."

"Of course," I stammered, "we failed to tell you all that much about ourselves and there is no way that you would know."

There was a long silence as I deliberated about the true nature of my call.

"Father" I finally managed to say, "I was really intrigued by the line of your questions when we were interrupted by the accident. Would it be too much of an imposition if I came to talk with you again?"

"Of course, not" he replied. "I have some free time next week. I must be about my worship services on Sunday and tomorrow is filled with meetings already. Are you available on Tuesday afternoon?"

I calculated how long that would be in terms of Mothers' request, knowing that I was not going to blow her off and then agreed with the time.

"That sounds doable for me," I said "How is two o'clock?"

"That would be excellent, Doctor Livingston"

"Thank you" I replied.

"Good night and thank you for calling." He said, "I will be sure and let my housekeeper know of your concern."

"Good bye and thank you". I said no longer feeling angry or smart.

With that information firmly in place I immediately dialed another number. Again, there was a long period of ringing. Then a voice came on the line.

"Hello, Livingston's." The voice said

"Mother," I said. "This is Devon. How are you?"

"Well, hello" she answered. "I did not expect to get a call from you. Did you get my wire?"

"Yes, I did. That's why I'm calling."

"Please, Devon" the voice hardened. "Don't tell me you're not coming."

"No" I put on my best adult voice, "I can come but I'm doing a research project and I only have the weekend available. Could we possibly do Paris tomorrow?"

"Tomorrow!" she sounded aghast.

"I have to be back in Rabat by 1PM on Tuesday." I tried to make it sound as official as I felt it was, not just a question-and-answer period about a personal religion. Mother would never have accepted that as a reasonable excuse.

"Well," she hesitated and then came a sigh, "all right, Devon, I do have a clear weekend so shall we say… meet at the hotel in Paris by tomorrow evening?"

"Sure, Mother." I answered. Then there was a click. She hung up once her end of the business was finished. Not a woman of many words, she got the business done and that was that.

I immediately called the airline and booked my flight. Next, I dialed the number Mother had given me to her choice of hotels in Paris. It was all very quick and painless. A phone call, a credit card, all very impersonal, I began to pack as my flight would leave for Paris in time to arrive at 3PM the next day. No big rush, just the usual orderly movement through time. I would not inform Tanemghurt of my weekend away as she should be traveling by car back to her home in Adrar, a trip that I believed would take a number of days. By the time she arrived at her home I could be back in Rabat for my meeting with the priest.

The flight to Paris was uneventful. I had visited there before and found the city charming but not really to my liking. I have heard so many people ramble on about its' great beauty and romantic atmosphere, but it just always left me a little cold. Mother liked to stay near the university in the Latin Quarter so the accommodations were old but very nice. I checked in, asked if Mother had arrived and was informed that she was expected soon. I knew she would be taking the Euro rail from London. The next order of business was the clothes shopping. I was expected to dress properly while in the city; no bohemian skirts or work clothes. I was to look the part of HER daughter.

That is the way it is for me. I will play the part, resenting it all the time I'm doing it. I had tried in those early college days to be myself a little more but that had brought the cold stare and the shunning silence from Mother. If I was going to live in her home; I would consent to follow her idea about how a young woman was to appear.

I think that was the hurtful part of it all. It was only an appearance that was required. Even as I toured the clothing stores making selections, I could feel myself growing angry. In Tanemghurt's family and even in the prejudicial homes in Morocco I had been able to be myself. I may have resented Janine's bossy ways but I could not feel angry. This was my real family, my only living parent and I would rather not be in her presence. I decided on two outfits and then returned to the hotel.

I sat near the window of my hotel room sipping the tea I had ordered through room service. I just did not feel like going out. As if from far away, I began to hear the sing song of Tanemghurt's voice as she translated:

"Salvation is that which makes us human

Takes us from darkness and into the light

Moves us from chaos, despair and destruction

Puts us in place with God as our love

Salvation changes the way that we view things

Humbles and gladdens our hearts and our minds

Makes us a bridge instead of a fencepost

Gives us a vision of who we can be"

Tanemghurt said that once we are saved, we will begin to forgive, first others and then eventually ourselves. I knew I was angry at my mother; I even knew why. Perhaps now would be a good time to forgive her. I was not assuming I had been saved but the thought of forgiving felt good. I played a scene in my mind to see how it might feel; but when I told the mental image of Mother my feelings, she locked me in her icy stare and flashed a small smile that involved only her mouth. It was her way of dismissing me. It hurt all over again.

Suddenly the phone rang. It was the senior desk clerk letting me know that Doctor Livingston had arrived and would meet me in the main lobby promptly at 6 PM. She could not have made that call herself, I supposed. I replaced the receiver and began to dress. Time would pass and soon I would know what she wanted of me. I was a block of wood hoping the axe did not cut away too much.

I rode the elevator down and arrived at five minutes to six. A little early with time to loiter was preferable to being late. I took a seat on a small settee with a good view of the elevators. Promptly at six PM the center doors parted and out stepped a superbly dressed older woman who looked remarkably like photos I had seen of my grandfather on my mother's side. Suddenly I realized it was my mother aged beyond what I had expected to see. Her hair, always impeccably colored was now snow white. Her skin, once flawless and filled with cosmetics was now sallow and wrinkled. The bearing once stern and regal was now stooped and slow. The eyes were the same. Still steely and judgmental, that was how I knew it was she. I rose to greet her and my confusion showed as she extended her hand to me, a gesture I had not seen her perform before.

"Devon, darling," she began. "How ever are you, my dear?" She leaned forward in a mock hug a little like that witnessed at Hollywood award shows. Sort of showing one cares without actually having to make contact with another human being.

"I…I'm fine, Mother" I stammered. "How are you?"

"I can tell by your look that you see I am not really well." She was breathing heavily as she walked leaning against my offered hand. "We must come and sit, talk for awhile. Have you eaten yet? You do look a bit thin." There it was… the phony English accent. She was a Midwesterner just like Dad and me. She must have watched a few hundred old films to get the accent just right.

We traveled across the lobby to a pair of overstuffed armchairs placed in a quiet alcove. Mother sat with a deep sigh. We would find food but not until she had rested.

"I see that you continue to bear the wounds of your adventure. Is it painful?" She wanted to be concerned but was not stopping for answers to her questions.

"As you can see" she rambled on, "I am not a well woman. I have been in hospital recently. It was only a short stay this time but it does so disrupt my research work. I try very hard not to let it but, I seem not to have control over it."

"Mother" I interrupted, "can you tell me what is wrong with you?" It seemed a small request.

"Cancer" she mouthed the word without actually speaking out loud. It was not a pleasant thought by any means but then it is a disease we are learning to fight. I nodded but decided not to comment, at least not now.

"You say you have been hospitalized?" I was trying to make some sense of things.

"Well, I was not going to bother you with it, dear." She began her regal pious tone. "You're being so busy with your career and all." Was that supposed to be an accusation of guilt? "We are made of sterner stuff than that. Truly, dear, may we now journey to the restaurant for a small supper?"

"Of course, we can." I rose and offered my hand which she actually accepted, being careful not to touch the bandages that still traveled up my arm. There was a fine little dining room adjacent to the lobby that offered a continental cuisine. We were seated immediately and began our version of small talk. All of it was about her work at the research center, her nights at opera or ballet, and her intimate evenings with at least fifty of her dearest friends; all so unimportant to me. Names and titles were important for her; count so and so or duchess of whoville. It didn't matter, as long as it sounded regal and above the average person, she loved it. I had long ago given up trying to wedge a word into her train of thought. She was impressive in her ability to turn any subject into a discussion about herself and her own life. I suppose I had also given up listening to it.

She was actually able to order, receive the meal, and eat with very little disruption of her story line. She was like American news cast with only herself as the subject. She left out nothing including dialogue as well as her internal thoughts as the scene was playing out.

Finally, the dinner ended and we walked toward the elevators.

"Mother" I began in the brief silence, "I'm still not sure exactly why I had to fly to Paris to see you. All that you have told me so far, except for the health issue, could have been a phone conversation."

She rolled her eyes and sighed. I was immediately sorry for breaking into her monologue; it always seemed to extend the time needed to finish what she had to say. A silence began to stretch between us as the elevator doors opened. We entered and found we were alone.

"I know I have been a bit secretive, Devon." She sounded surprisingly emotional. "Really I know that, but I just don't know how to tell you some things." She turned to face me and for possibly the second time in my life I realized that I was taller than my mother. She had always been so overpowering and impressive; I had always felt small.

"Devon," she began "you are my child. My parents are gone, my brother died in the military and you are my family. Now I am about to die and I don't want to be without you anymore. Is that foolish?"

"No, Mother." I wanted to take her hand but the elevator stopped and the doors opened. "Would you like for me to come with you for awhile?"

"Yes, please" she stumbled slightly and I reached for her. "I am alright but I would like a bit of company."

We walked slowly down the hall to her suite. I knew that her parents had passed away of various diseases before I was born but this was the first I had heard of an uncle. Although I was curious and shocked, I knew to keep calm and wait for the news. She was probably unaware that I had never heard of him. I calculated that this brother may have died during the Vietnam conflict, if he had been near her age. She had always appeared to believe that she was the center of the universe and therefore, anything she knew, was obvious to those she lived with since she must be the object of our total concern. We unlocked the door and entered the living area. The suite was gorgeous, nothing but the best for my mother. She had worked for some of her wealth and she liked to acknowledge that fact in the way that she chose to live.

Once again, we found a pair of wing back chairs to sit facing one another.

"Mother" I began, "can you tell me exactly what the doctors are telling you? We are alone now and I would like to know."

"Yes, Devon, I shall." She laid her head against the back of the chair and closed her eyes for a moment. I held my silence knowing that sharing the less than beautiful parts of her life were difficult, especially for Mother. Always appearing to me as a self sufficient, independent person; Dad said they parted ways because she simply did not need him. I always felt that she didn't need me either.

"As I have indicated" she began, "I have been battling cancer, colon cancer to begin with, which is often curable, but it has moved around and has metastasized to several internal organs, most of them vital. I had surgery two years ago, which I am sorry I did not tell you about. I know it was selfish of me, I see that now. I just can't seem to…" Words began to fail and a tear rolled down one cheek.

"I know, Mom." I'd never called her that before but I was glad I did because it made her smile. She produced a handkerchief from her purse and wiped the tear away. It was a linen hanky, monogrammed in soft pink threads, a remnant of a nearly ancient past.

"Devon," she said "I've so much to tell you. I always wanted to tell you these things but I thought I would have more time; there would always be a tomorrow. Now I know that tomorrow has come and so I'm going to get this out of the way as best I can."

I settled in to listen and encourage as my mother finally shared the story of her life through her eyes. I had heard my father's version and several of the faculty members at the university knew her but still this was an outsiders' view; a side that I had not seen until this night.

"Devon" she began "I want you to know first, that I have always loved you. I know that I am often distant with you but I do care immensely for you."

This was hard for me to hear but I held my tongue and let the anger pass.

"I know you have wanted what was best, Mother." I tried to be adult and leave the past in the past.

"No, I haven't, Devon," she shook her head, "I've been awful and I need to tell you how I feel."

"The past is over" I offered, "We can just go on from here."

"No" she insisted her voice growing stronger, "I must have the truth out."

"Before you were born," she continued, "your father and I were very much in love. I thought we had the world ahead of us and that nothing could ever spoil our life. We were young and beautiful and well educated. We had such a large circle of friends, all young and in love with life just as we were. Then you came along. Your Father absolutely adored you. It was as if I no longer existed in his eyes, as if your entrance into the world overshadowed me. Devon, I am sorry." She began to cry and her English accent began to fall away. "You were just a tiny, helpless baby but I was actually jealous of you." I wanted to say something but no thoughts appeared in my shock at her admittance.

"When we had married, I had vowed that I would help your father finish his business degree. He was not one to apply himself totally to any project and the four years drug out to six. You were two years old when I made my decision to leave; he had finally completed the degree and started to work for a prestigious firm. I briefly took the role of dutiful wife but it was so horrible. I demanded to be given the freedom to work on my own agendas but he really did not seem to care whether I stayed or left. So, I took the one thing that I knew would hurt him the most…I took you."

"I don't remember any of that," I protested. "I can't see how it matters now…"

"Please, Devon," she commanded "it will all become apparent soon. I suppose it was my leaving that drove him into the arms of that Shelly woman. She was so beneath us all you know." I closed my eyes to prevent her from seeing them roll in irritation.

"It was that news of Alexander's death that prompted me to send you back to your Father's home. Our parents had passed away the year following your birth and their insurance policies had accrued equally to my brother and me. Alexander, my hero, was in the Navy so he had willed all his remaining assets to me. It was horrible, the news of his passing in that unpopular war. The grief that I bore, the pain, the money was of little account to me. Then I realized that I could complete my studies with the monies I had been given. Alexander would have approved. There was nothing left but to return you to your father so that my deceased brother's dreams might be accomplished." This had to be the most dramatic piece of history I had ever heard; then she continued.

Mother had always insisted that she had been raised in an academic atmosphere. The reality was that she and her older brother Alexander had lived at a parochial boarding school in the upper Midwest where her father was the handy man and her mother worked in the kitchen. They were allowed to attend classes at this school but all the children knew they were the servants' children and this left both of them feeling quite inferior. Mother indicated that this was a source of her need to compete scholastically.

I found myself feeling a little less angry and located a sense of pity for my mother. She had endured much but there was something that seemed missing. She was apologizing to me for leaving me as a small child but where was she as I grew up within my family; a family that did not include anyone who admitted being related to her? Dad always made excuses for the lack of gifts on birthdays and Christmas but I didn't even remember phone calls in those early years.

"You know, dear," she seemed to read my mind "I did my very best to allow you the freedom to develop your life with your father's new family. I wanted only the best for you and a single mother; even in that day was a creature more to be pitied than praised."

"Turn it around to you" I thought. It was still all about her. On the other hand, I did have more information than ever before. Dad always answered my questions about her but they were short and given to a young child who could not be expected to understand the intricacies of love and relationships. Others, who probably knew, seemed reluctant to speak as if they too were overwhelmed by her mere presence.

Suddenly she sighed. "Devon, might we meet in the morning? I have grown quite weary from the travel. We could gather at the little bistro for brunch, say ten-ish?"

"Sure" I kept the answer short and rose to make my exit. "Thanks for telling me, I know it was hard. If you need me, you know my room number."

She extended her hand once again and I took it in passing. It was ice cold. Somehow that seemed appropriate.

I returned to my simple room and prepared for bed but sleep would not come. We become who we are based on nature as well as nurture. A lot of who I am is reflective of my dad and stepmom but some of it came from her too. I vaguely remembered living in a place without my dad; there were lots of faces, babysitters I guess, but his face was among them so I know he came to visit. She had to have worked and that would have put other people in charge of me. My main young memory of Mother was the picture my Father insisted that I keep on the bureau in my room. It was a classic pose of a woman with very dark hair and hazel eyes that seemed to look right through me. That was Mother and "that Shelly woman" was the person I always called Mom.

I remembered my life growing up now and the loving, giving, arguing, and ordinary family I had been given after Mother went away. My Dad sold insurance for awhile and then worked for an advertising agency. Shelly worked away from home sometimes but not far away from us. When my sisters were small, she ran a daycare in our home and when they went to school, she took a job working in the kitchen there. She was always present for us. I guess when I was young, I always saw her as my parent and the woman in the picture as some foreign person I was obliged to recognize. When my dad and sisters died, I thought I would die too. I wanted to die. If it hadn't been for Shelly needing me to be there for her, I might have done something to make that happen. I was a teenager and gave Shelly a ton of grief. I argued and fought and often felt angry toward her for no reason but she never let me down in those days.

I wondered what my mother thought when Dad and the twins died? I knew she had sent flowers because Shelly was quick to point that out, as if that meant she really cared. The truth as I knew it now is that it was the appropriate thing to do, Mother would always do the appropriate thing. Maybe the deaths in her family had hardened her, or caused her to become so terribly self-centered.

I prepared for bed and looked around for something to read. I had packed so absent-mindedly that I had forgotten to throw in a book. I usually travel with one but this had been a terribly reflective day and I found myself without my routine. The gift shop was closed and I was too tired to go out into the Parisian night to look for anything new. I turned to the bedside table and found a book titled the Holy Bible in French. I thought this seemed odd but then remembered seeing them in lots of hotel rooms as I traveled in my undergrad years. I was told there was an international society that went around placing the books in rooms for people to pick up and read. As a young coed I thought it was weird but now I welcomed the distraction.

I read and dozed off and on through the night. I was not great at French but I knew enough to figure it out. The stories I had heard discussed recently all had to do with the new part of the book but as I flipped absently through the old part, I found lots of interesting things there also. I had always heard about this book but had never had the time to actually read any of it before. At six AM I noticed the sun beginning to rise and decided to make a call to someone I hadn't spoken to in some time. I dug out my address book, checked the time and calculated the hour in the United States, then dialed. The voice that answered was pleasingly familiar.

"Hello", she said.

"Hello, Shelly?" I was trembling. "It's me Devon."

"Well, honey," she nearly shouted. "How in the world are you? Are you okay? I hadn't talked to you since Lord knows when. Where are you, baby?"

"Oh, I'm fine." my eyes welled with tears. "I guess I just needed to hear a happy voice. How are you?"

"Finer th'n frogs' hair" she drawled. Shelly was originally from Texas and never let her heritage slip away. Where Mother faked an English accent, Shelly presented an honest Southern American drawl. "I promise to be as happy as you need me to be. What's going on?"

"I'm not sure, actually." I tried not to let the tears show in my voice. "I am in Paris right now. I got a call from my mother. She asked me to meet and talk with her and now she says she is dying of cancer." I had not meant for it all come rolling out like that but I just could not be grown up for this small instant.

"Oh, honey," she said "I am so sorry. That's so much for my little girl to bear. I got your letter about being in the hospital in Africa and I mailed you one back but I bet you haven't got it yet. I hadn't heard from you in so long I just loved your letter. Can I give you a big old hug through the phone?" She was talking to me as if I was fifteen years old and it felt good. All the silence and the mean teenaged words had not changed her attitude toward me.

"You always know what to say." I responded. "Actually, what I really need now are some adult answers to questions I never wanted to ask. Some things that may not be my business but I need to know about my past from someone with no reason to turn it into something it's not."

"Okay" she sounded doubtful.

"Did you know Mother before?" I had to know the reality of her relationship with my parents.

"Before what, honey?" Shelly asked.

"Before she and Daddy divorced." I suspected the answer but now I needed the truth. There was a long pause before she answered.

"No, baby," she said. "I didn't know them but I knew of them. They ran in the fast crowd. Your Mom and Dad they were college students at the University, the one you graduated from. They were students and they acted like folks who had a lot of money to burn. It was the sixties. Your Dad was always cutting class to be at the rallies and peace marches, that's why he took a little extra time to get through. Your Mom was a society person, or at least she told everyone that she was. I worked at a restaurant called the Dove back in those days. I was just a regular little old' waitress finishing high school and wishing I could go to that college. You know my folks lived there in town but your Daddy was from Kansas. I really don't know where your mother was born; it was like I met her at the Dove and never wanted to know much more. Actually, that's where they got your name. They wanted to call you Dove but that sounded odd so your mom came up with Devon."

"They named me after a restaurant?" I was a little shocked. "She told me I was named after a county in England."

"Well sure" she was on a roll, "everybody was doing that, naming their kids after the places they were conceived. It was just a thing…" It must have been my silence that stopped her. "Devon, I'm sorry. I didn't really know your Mama; your dad and I only had a few necessary conversations about her. I don't want to carry gossip."

"No" I stammered, "I want truth, Shelly. My parents were real people not the good old gang from some TV sitcom. They ate and drank and for all I know did drugs." There was that silence again. "The truth, Shelly… Mom… please." The sigh she sent me was unmistakable, I had happened upon a truth, a painful one.

I learned that my parents were no angels. They had been part of a very wild crowd known for parties and pot smoking. The political activism seemed to go hand in hand with all that back then. My Mother had a reputation as a rather promiscuous girl. The break up Mother had blamed on her need for independence was more likely caused by my dad finding her in the arms of another man. At least that was the story he told my stepmother when they first started dating. Shelly had tended to disbelieve that until she saw the divorce decree among the papers she found when he died. They did not have a no-fault law in those days. Dad had sued Mother on grounds of marital disaffection. He won his case but lost custody of me. They moved to Kansas to get away from her and the gossip she seemed to carry with her.

"What about this brother I never heard of? A man named Alexander who died in the Vietnam War?" I asked.

"Well, she did have a brother in the Navy but he died in San Francisco about a year after you were born, that's when she changed her name."

"Her what?" now I was truly shocked. "Her name is not Alexis Livingston?"

"No, actually, her name is Anna Ruth. Her brothers' name was Alex and when he died, she took to calling herself Alexis saying it was in his honor. You were already born and named so she couldn't rename you but she did try. I don't mean to put her down, but I never understood your mother; we all thought she would end up on the stage somewhere giving wonderful performances because she was such a good actress."

That was it. That was the thing about my mother that I could not quite grasp. She was playing a part even greater than the one she asked me to play in her presence.

"There was something your Daddy once told me" Shelly broke into my thoughts, "he said that actors who don't act on a stage have a problem dealing with other people. They can control the emotions they present to the world but they can't control anybody else in the scene. It's like there is no script so they have to make it all up as they go along. She's very smart, Devon, very smart."

"What did she really do when Daddy died, Mom?" I needed to know no matter how difficult the answer.

"Oh, Lord, Devie," she used my baby name and I was immediately sorry for bringing it up. "That was such a hard time. I don't remember some things but I do remember her. She showed up wearing a black dress with a veil over her face like she was still married to your dad. Folks said she was trying to look like Jackie Kennedy. She made a spectacle of herself at the funeral home hanging on the arm of some guy we never saw before or since. I had other stuff on my mind that day. I guess we never have much talked about it, though.”

“I know, Mom,” I said “I’m sorry.”

“No, no,” she replied, “this needs to be talked about. I know we all take times in our lives when we just have to think about where we been before we can see where we’re going.” She was so smart, my mom. So not beneath anybody in the world, I had been so angry at her when I left home, I could not see straight. I suddenly wished I had been able to see the beauty of that family I had been part of. In some ways they had been just like Tanemghurt’s family.

“When Daddy and the girls died,” I now approached the other topic, “how did you know where to go for the church service? I don’t remember us going to church a lot or even at all until after that.”

There was a pause before she began.

“That was another thing about your dad” Shelly began “he wasn’t much one for church but he had this idea that we were all religious or God believers somewhere deep down. His folks, who you never got a chance to meet, were real holy rollers. He told me his Mama dragged him to church twice a week until he was old enough to drive and then he started in to lying to her about where he was during the meetings. It wasn’t that he didn’t believe but I think he just got tired of being told what to believe. He never took you to church because he didn’t want you to feel the same way. His parents were pretty wealthy and disowned him when things got cross ways between your Mama and his. He still ended up with some property in the end but that could never fix the hard feelings. I have a cousin in the same church your Daddy’s parents were members of, so that’s how I got hold of that minister. Your Dad had sort of walked away from God but in the end, I knew I had to take him home.”

“Well,” I said “it was a beautiful service, at least, the parts I remember.”

“Yup” she chuckled, “for the parts I remember too. Are you better now?”

“I think so,” I replied. “Am I keeping you from something?”

“Lord no, Devon,” she said. “Honey, I’d rather talk to you than anyone in this world. When I lost my little girls and their Daddy, I wanted to go with them. If you hadn't been around…well, I don't know."

"I know," I offered "I have thought the same thing more than once. Without you, I'm sure I would have given up. Why did you send me to live with my mother after graduation?"

Shelly sounded a little shocked. "Well, I thought your Mama told you. We all wanted you to go to college and that was a good one. She helped get you the scholarship that put you through your undergrad studies."

"No, she didn't" I replied. Now I knew a truth I could share. "Her boyfriend, the guy she was living with, paid for me to go to college for the first year. After that I won some scholarships and worked, mostly at the Dove. She did give me some money but she said it was a pension from my dad's accounts. Something you controlled and she wasn't always happy with the amounts you sent."

"Well," Shelly replied slowly, "there was a fund your dad had setup that paid for some of your living expenses and I was the one who sent it. Only I sent it to her because she said you moved around a lot and she would be better able to get it to you on time. How much did you receive? I'm just curious."

"It seemed to vary" I remembered "some months it was a few hundred and the next it might be only seventy-five to eighty dollars. It always seemed odd that the amount changed. She said it was interest on an account and the variances were tied to the interest rate. It sorts of made sense to me at the time."

"Good Lord," she exploded. "We got ourselves bamboozled on that one. It was the same seven hundred and fifty dollars every month summer and winter until you graduated from college. That woman is still a weasel. I'm sorry Devon, I shouldn't say mean things but she is a mean woman."

"Well," I was too tired to be angry, "it was a long time ago. I guess I'm too tired to care about the ugly things people can do to one another."

There was a prolonged silence before I came up with what I wanted to say next.

"I'm sorry, Mom," I kept my voice as even as possible as the tears began to fall. "All these years I have wasted hating you. I'm so sorry."

"Oh, Devon," the voice returned, "please, don't cry. It's not easy being a stepmom and some of the misdirected anger is part of the territory. I know you didn't really hate me. Some days I wasn't really fond of you either and I'm sorry for that. A little kid can't be anymore than she is and you were just being a regular little kid caught in a windstorm."

"I wasn't a little kid when Dad died though and that's when I was the worst." All the pain of losing came back. "I was so mean to you when I was in high school. Some part of me even tried to blame you for the accident."

"Some part of me blamed me too." She whispered. Her voice came back as she remembered, "I had my support system though. The other Mom's of your classmates were and are some of my best friends. A couple of them had lost husbands too and were struggling to keep their families together. Some were divorced and one had her hubby just up and walk away. She never did find him."

"Well, that really stinks" I replied.

"At least we always knew where your Daddy was..." Shelly's voice trailed and I heard her sobbing. I wished desperately that I could be there to hug her and tell her the words I had heard in the cave. "To one who suffers pain, He is compassion".

"I love you, Mom," I said through tears.

"I love you too, baby girl. You call me again any time you want."

"I will, Mom. I'm sending you a big hug."

"Oh, that's the best. Bye now, I love you." I could hear her sobs.

"Bye". The line hummed as I hung up. That was the appropriate way to end a conversation. In a few hours I would be expected to appear for another command performance. Life for me had slowed down. I felt as though I had time to think about where I had been instead of always racing off looking for the next place to go. I drifted off to sleep until the ringing of the phone jarred me into wakefulness.

"Devon?" it was Mother, "would it seem awful of me to ask you to come to my suite for brunch? I'm still feeling rather drawn I'm afraid."

"Of course, not" I answered grabbing the bedside clock, "that might even make it all the better for personal conversation. What time would you like for me to arrive."

There was a long silence, then "Well, certainly. I…I am ready any time you are. Is there anything in particular I can order for us?"

"No Mother" I said, "whatever you decide will be perfect. I'll be there in a few minutes then."

Again, the line hummed in the abrupt ending. I stretched and peeked through the curtains into the French morning sunshine. It felt like a very different day.

When I arrived at Mothers' suite the door was ajar. I tapped lightly and then pushed it open to reveal the busboy leaning over a small slumped figure in a dressing gown. He had the phone to one ear and was screaming something in French into the receiver. It took me a few moments to realize that the figure was my mother and he was calling for medical help. I entered and waited for him to finish the conversation. She looked so small now. Less than thirty minutes had passed since our conversation.

The young man turned to me and began in French, and then realizing I was American began to question me in broken English. I explained that this was my mother and that I had come to meet with her. I told him about her illness and with each passing sentence he became more silent and reserved. Just as I finished my last sentence the door flung wide behind me and the hotel manager along with an EMT crew arrived. I was questioned and asked for identification but the concierge was well aware of parts of our story so there was little for them to question. It was determined that Mother had indeed passed away from what appeared to be a massive heart attack. The hotel staff was very compassionate and tried to help in any way they could. Oddly, I felt nothing. I felt cold and flat as I spoke with each official.

Medical records were sent for from England; fortunately, Mother's long conversation the previous day, along with records she carried in her personal property provided us with enough information to give the authorities all they needed to know. The next two days were spent with more officials and a decision was made to have the body cremated so that I could do with the remains as I wished. It was all so clinical. I remember one young secretary looking at me closely and then speculating that I had been angry with my mother at the time of her demise. I smiled and nodded rather than get into any long explanations. I was not angry or hurt, in fact, I felt nothing at all.

Paris was once again all I had ever found it to be, lovely to look at but not a place I wanted to remain. Fall was coming and the trees were just beginning to turn. The air would continue to cool until winter arrived as it always did. The cremation could not happen quickly. There were papers to sign and the process itself was rather long. I offered that I would have to leave to complete business in Morocco but then I would return to pick up the remains and take them to England for proper burial. Somehow, I knew that Mother would have wanted it that way. I did call the research institute where she had an office but there was no answer. I assumed the weekend had been extended for some unknown reason since it was Monday but left a message for someone to contact me at their earliest convenience on my cell number.

I headed back to Morocco early Tuesday morning, knowing I would arrive in plenty of time for my meeting with Fr. Christian. I wanted to share all this with someone.

CHAPTER 11
INTO THE NIGHT

The sound of the elevator at the end of the hallway broke the rhythm of her story. I glanced at my watch and realized it was nearly eleven. We would have to make a decision about where to continue the story very soon.

"Hi folks," it was Cam, the building security guard, "this all-nighter we're pullin' in here?"

"Hello, Cam" I stood and stretched by back. "Oh, I don't know."

"Well, if you do, you folks turn out the light as you leave." He smiled and began his instruction. "The hall lights stay on until midnight, then they go on relays that only light up when there's movement in the hall. I'll be around 'tween here and the next two buildin's so if you need anything…"

"I have your security number" I indicated my cell phone neatly strapped to my waist.

"Y'all be good now," he grinned in a grandfatherly way and tipped his hat. "Good night, Doctor Livingston, Doctor Hanesworthy."

"Good night, Cam" Devon said without turning around.

He closed the door and we were left with silence.

"Well," I began wanting her to make the choice, "what shall we do? I suppose that's license for us to remain as we are or to choose something else." I hesitated hoping she could read my mind. The tear drifting down her cheek sent me crumpling into the sofa next to her.

"Devon," I curled her into my arms "whatever is going on? Is it…"

"Oh," she sniffed "it's just me. I suddenly missed my mom."

"You mean her, your mother…"

"No, my mom," she pulled away a bit, "Shelly, she died two weeks ago and talking about our last conversation… I guess it just hit me. She was my rock, my dad connection, and now they are both gone.”

She suddenly sat upright and patted my hand and sniffed. “I’m fine. Just needed to shed one more tear, I guess.”

“I’m so sorry to hear that.” We were obviously not going anywhere for a while. I took her hand in both of mine and she did not pull away. Her hand was surprisingly soft for an archaeologist. “Well,” I thought “just how many archaeologists hands have you held?” I looked into the deep blue eyes and did not turn away.

“She died of colon cancer.” She shook her head slowly. “I went to the hospital three days before she died but she wasn’t able to talk to me. I got to hold her hand and read to her, she had a book of poems my dad had written; another thing I knew nothing about. They were mostly love poems, I’m sure he wrote them for her.”

“That must have been very difficult.” I sympathized.

“No actually,” she said brightening somewhat with each sentence, “it was comforting for me. When Mother died it was if I didn’t care but with Shelly, I got to have closure with her as a person. I got to plan the funeral, we had a nice church service, buried her in a very pretty cemetery; and I even got to meet my dad’s younger sister. I had heard of Aunt Dory but I guess the split with my dad and his folks probably had some impact on that relationship. Anyway, she was really nice and helpful. They all lived in that same small town in Kansas and rarely spoke to one another. I wish I had been able to know them all better when I was young.”

“I’m sure,” I said, “family, even if it’s rowdy like mine, is a great comfort. In times of crises, we do need people to lean on and family members always seem to know us best. Hard to fool an older sister who remembers what a slob you were in elementary school.”

“That sounds personal” she said leaning back on the pillows behind her. The tears had dried and she was smiling again.

“It is.” I relaxed, “when I was married to Helen, one of the things she complained about was my inability to help with the housework. We both taught so she felt I should perform some of the cleaning at home. When I shared this with my sister, she nearly had a fit laughing. Said I was a slob in third grade and she knew I would never be able to keep a tidy place.”

"So, are you?" Devon grinned "a slob, I mean."

"Oh definitely" I said "on the scale of slobdom, I'd say I'm a master."

Devon laughed; it was almost musical. She was delightful; very pretty and delightful. I wondered if I was falling in love. More specifically, could she be falling in love with me? I wondered if I might kiss her and began to move toward her. She looked away, toward the picture window now dark with night. Our reflections stared back at us in the glow of the overhead lights.

"Tell you what, Freddie," she patted my hand which had purposely fallen on her knee, "let's go out and drive around. You have a convertible, don't you?" Devon rose from the couch out of my reach.

"Yes," I mumbled in response to that baby name. Her mood and demeanor had quite suddenly changed and we were to be happy again.

"It should be a really nice night." She began to put the objects of our repast into the basket again. "We could drive for awhile, if that's okay with you?"

"Alright," I sounded peppier than I felt as I rose "but only if you promise to continue the story. How about your mother's place in England? Did you meet with the priest again? How about your Amazigh friend? Oh right, you said she's actually coming here."

We bounded into the hall way stopping to flip off the light as our custodian had requested. Moved on to the elevator and a short trip down, then, out into the warm evening air. It was magnificent. The sky was clear and a full moon washed the campus in light.

"Oh, my, gosh," Devon enthused "can you smell that. It's like a perfume explosion out here."

I breathed in the deeply scented air and easily agreed. Fortunately, this time I knew where I needed to be when I parked my car so it was waiting patiently just outside the Union doors in one of the slots marked for faculty only. Normally, I do not use them as it seems a bit divisive, but tonight was a special occasion. Devon plumped the basket in the back seat and I held the door for her to enter. We were smiling and silly as we moved away into the night. I had no idea where we were going and for once in my frightened little life; I did not care. The moon was full and bright overhead and stars appeared at the edges of the horizon.

The engine turned over and immediately my radio began to play, it was one of my favorite Beatles songs. I reached to turn it off and Devon touched my hand.

"I love this song," she grinned as I backed out of the slot.

"Me too" I grinned back. "I was only a kid when they were around but it was all I heard in my Mum's house." I gunned the motor slightly.

"Oh, drive slow," she breathed "I want us to smell the flowers while we drive."

I smiled and carefully held my speed to the recommended limit on campus. The air was warm for spring and the wash of moonlight made the night as bright as day. We worked our way to the end of the long drive and sat poised between two brick and mortar gateposts. The choice of roads at the intersection was left or right as a forward choice would have landed us in the living room of the delta epsilon sorority house. I looked at my companion as she looked at me.

"Let's go left." We both announced at the same time followed by laughing. So, we rode for nearly a half an hour listening to the music, a Beatles anthology, soon we found ourselves rolling along a two-lane blacktop some-where in the country outside the university town. I'd been having visions of Audrey Hepburn in a flowing white scarf sitting next to me when Devon's voice broke in.

"Fred," she questioned leaning toward me, "do you have any idea where we are?"

"Well, actually no." I answered. "I know we've come along a state highway that's well traveled. I believe we'll end up in another small town soon. Did you need anything?"

"No," she answered "but if you get a chance, I might like to stop and stretch my legs."

The lights of a small town in a valley twinkled on the horizon.

"How about there?" I questioned.

"Sure." Devon answered.

As we rolled into the village, I realized that conversation such as we had shared at the school was nearly impossible on the road. The sound of the radio aided by the wind seemed to whisk each word off into the moon drenched night and thwarted any attempt at communication. The only answer was to find a place to stop. Just as I was pondering the possibilities, an all-night diner appeared in the distance. I glanced at my passenger and she nodded her approval.

The café was small and totally void of anyone save a single waitress scrubbing at a countertop. She raised her head in acknowledgement of our presence and we took a booth near the door. At least the place smelled clean and the quiet was essential for our continuing the story. We ordered coffees and water before she could arrive to lay down menus. A shrug without remark was her only response as she turned to fetch the items.

I boldly took Devon's hand and this time she did not resist.

"Okay" I stared deeply into her eyes, "are we ready to continue?"

"Are you sure you want to hear all this," she demurred.

I raised my right hand.

"Devon, I swear I am in this to the end. I am hooked."

Devon laughed and shook her head.

"How else am I going to be able to help you write all this down?" I questioned. "C'mon, I can take it. Unless you are totally making this up…"

She shook her head, "Truly, I wish I was." She squinted her eyes at me and let out a long sigh. "What I can't figure out is why I'm telling you all of this. I know you asked but I don't normally dump on people the way I did on you at the lounge."

"Perhaps I am just such a wonderful guy you couldn't help yourself," we both giggled at the thought. I was still allowed to hold her hand as the coffees came and she began.

CHAPTER 12
SURPRISES

The flight to Morocco was happily uneventful. It was actually good to get away from all the death and compassion I was experiencing in Paris. The people I encountered at the hotel all knew about Mother and the fact that I was there by myself. Somehow it all seemed to be too much for some of them to bear. I would see the maids whispering as I passed in the hall and even the receptionists would smile sadly and nod. I wanted to turn to them and explain that some strange part of me was almost pleased to have her forever gone from my life. Of course, I didn't, that would not be appropriate.

From the airport I hailed a taxi and gave the driver the address of the church. He looked at me questioningly and I remembered it was fall and the beginning of Ramadan. I was dressed appropriately to visit my mother rather than in the drab clothing I had been choosing to wear during my days with Tanemghurt. As the driver pulled away from the airport, I flipped open my cell phone and randomly dialed. I began a fake conversation in French as if to let him think that I was in contact with someone who would miss me if I did not arrive on time. I made a second call, this time using the few phrases I knew of the Moroccan language on the small chance that he did not speak French, and introducing myself as Doctor Livingston. Maybe if he was suspicious of a woman, he might at least respect the title.

My journey was over rather quickly and we pulled to an abrupt stop in front of the church. I handed the driver the fare along with a sizable tip but he acted as if the cash might be contaminated. He clearly did not like dealing with me but would not turn down the money. I had left all but one carry-on bag at the hotel in Paris, knowing I would return there. I had no intentions of staying in this country any longer than absolutely necessary. I did not plan on meeting with Tanemghurt in person until I knew where the old Prophetess was actually located.

I walked past the church and headed toward the small house. As I rounded to the entrance, I saw evidence of the accident that had occurred last week. The car was gone but the wall remained cracked and the tire marks still pitted the flower bed leading up to the fractures that bore evidence of the vehicle. I walked slowly now studying the crash site and remembering the chaos of that day. "Salvation moves us from chaos to love". I heard the voice of Tanemghurt once again in my head. How does all this fit? I wondered. I always thought life was just one foot in front of the other mixed with happenstance and hard work.

Just as I was pondering the grooves in the earth; the door to the little house popped open and the large friendly form of Fr. Christian stood before me.

"Come, my dear," he motioned as he spoke in his heavy French accent, "do come in. It is very warm for this time of year. I am so happy to see you have arrived on perfect time for our meeting. How are you?"

"I am fine and you, Father Christian?" I spoke as I shook his hand and entered the small adobe-like building. The room was an entry way which had contained some wooden cabinets and sturdy seating places the last time I had been here. Now it was filled with luggage and boxes as if someone were moving.

"Ah, I am well," he said picking his way through the jumble, "just a little crowded at the moment. You see, I have been recalled to France. I leave in the morning for my home and then off to an assignment in a new place."

"Oh, my" I said, "I don't mean to interrupt this." I suddenly felt as if I were intruding on this persons' life and that all my questions were perhaps silly and unimportant.

"No, no, my dear, I am most pleased to visit with you." The priest said ushering me past the baggage and into the library where we had originally met. The shelves were now nearly bare and the plaster and broken tiles had been swept away. He pointed me to a small desk away from the debris site and took a chair on the other side.

"Please, I need to speak with you." He was holding his hands together as if in prayer and the big brown eyes seemed to dance. "You see, I have found some information for you concerning the person you were looking for – this ancient person?"

I had all but forgotten about the search, the reason for coming to find this place. I had been so wrapped up in the feelings, the drama and the words of the last few days; I had almost lost the point of our investigation.

"Oh, please Father Christian," I said, "I am really happy to hear anything you can tell me."

He shared with me that following my phone call he had indeed contacted the monastery at Benni Abbes that Tanemghurt and I had asked about, out of curiosity as much as anything. The Little Brothers of the Gospel did still exist there and he had been able to talk to one of them. Unfortunately, the person he spoke with was unaware of any visits with the Berber people; although he did share that a sister, a female member of a community of women who followed the same devotions, had been on a retreat in the desert near there and had been injured in some sort of accident. The entire community had been praying for her for over a month. The affable priest rocked with enthusiasm as he talked with his hands as well as his voice in that particularly French way of speaking.

This was it; the answers were coming. I asked for a name and of course about the miracles. Was it possible that she performed miracles? Suddenly the friendly cleric seemed to stop. He shuffled in his seat and began to wag his head.

"Please understand, Ms Doctor," he seemed to demure, "the subject of miracles is a very tricky one for the Catholic church. It is not that we do not teach that miracles happen. No, no far from the truth; but to say emphatically that a thing is a miracle… well, for us it is a long process. First one must prove that there was a true illness or problem, and then one must prove that the solution or remedy has occurred without the intervention of human beings. What you shared with me is not always accepted as being…"

"But', I interrupted "I am sure that Tanemghurt is telling the truth about her people and the things the woman said to me…"

"I understand," he said, "truly I do. It is just that for official Church purposes we must be cautious and err on the side of reality. I do not doubt the young woman but the Church has it reasons."

For the next two hours, the priest and I sat at the little desk as he attempted to answer my questions. Questions which became more about my own life and how a deity could fit into the world the way I envisioned it. It became very clear that the old hell and damnation form of religious teaching was no longer a large part of the theology offered by his church but it was still there. Fr. Christian spoke more of examples of the compassion of Christ and often compared it to the teachings of other great leaders and philosophers around the world. He spoke of modern day prophets and how the teachings of Christianity had changed the way the world operates over the last two thousand years.

In the end I did not tell him about my mother's death or the hard feelings I continued to deal with concerning her. Somehow it just didn't seem important to the moment. I had envisioned spending a week or more learning from this man but his immanent travel plans were sure to prevent anything like that from occurring. He handed me several small books about the teachings of the Church and hoped that I would find time to read them. He said they would answer many of my questions and although he had wished for a little more time, he was sure I would find what I was looking for.

I left the house and actually walked for several streets before I realized that I needed a plan for the evening. In my rush to be at the meeting I had totally failed to reserve a hotel room or plan for a flight back to Paris even though my mind had planned an extra day to check on Tanemghurt. Just as I was pondering my fate a young man stopped before me and bowed slightly.

"Miss Doctor," he began in halting English. "It is I, Fadil, the brother of Tanemghurt."

I was shocked and nearly grabbed his hand in gratitude but wisely held back.

"I am very glad to see you, Fadil." I spoke slowly. "Is Tanemghurt around?"

"Ah, Tanemghurt is at our home at Algeria. I remained to work with my uncle."

I was disappointed but not surprised.

"This place is not safe. I may take you to hotel or the home of my uncle?" he gestured toward the same black car he had been driving to pick us up last week. At first, I thought to refuse as it seemed to be so much trouble but I knew him to be a sincere man.

"Thank you." I set my mind on the present, "I would like to go to the hotel."

He deposited me nicely at the same hotel and steadfastly refused any money. I crossed my fingers and prayed that there would be one room for the night. The clerk remembered me and after a few minutes was able to find me a usable single room where I could rest and make phone calls to arrange my transportation back to France. It was a faster turnaround that I had antic-ipated but it was all I could do. Ramadan was in full swing and the presence of a single American woman seemed to grate on the nerves of many of the people I was encountering. As soon as the sun set, the feasting would begin. The season prescribed that believers eat only once each day and that the meal begin after dark. For some this would turn into a party and the streets were no place for me.

I locked the door to my little room determined not to go out until morning. Fr. Christian had provided us with a light snack of fruits and soft bread so I knew I would not be hungry soon. I rummaged through my bag and found my address book containing the phone numbers for Tanemghurt. I may not be able to see her but at least I would tell her about the meeting. I had thought of telling her brother but I was afraid I could not explain everything properly.

Just as I was preparing to dial the number my cell phone rang.

"Hello," I said into the phone.

"Hello," a strange voice with a British accent said, "I was given this number to try and reach a Dr. Devon Livingston. This is Alexander Livingston speaking."

"Yes," I answered curiously, "this is Devon. How may I help you?"

"Well," the voice said "I believe you may have some news of my mother. She was traveling on the continent this week."

"Your Mother?" I questioned.

"Yes, Ms Alexis Livingston," the voice came back.

"Your Mother?" I had not intended to question twice but the words just seemed to tumble out.

"Are you and she somehow related?" he asked.

"Yes," I answered breathlessly. "She was my mother." The silence that hummed between us was almost palpable. What could I possibly say, perhaps he had the wrong person, and maybe there was more than one Alexis. As soon as that thought reached my mind, I rejected it.

"Look… ah…look," I stammered, "Alexander, I don't think this is a conversation we can have over the phone. Where are you?"

"I'm at home," the voice said quietly. "That is, I am in London at the townhouse."

"Okay" I started to think again as the shock seemed to settle in, "I'm in Morocco right now. It will take me a few days to tie up some business ends and then I'll come to London. We can meet and… Alexander, may I ask a personal question, how old are you?"

"Ah, well," he stammered back, "I'm an adult. I happen to be twenty-five right now. How old are you? Not meaning to be personal."

The question was fair. "I'm thirty-three." I suddenly had a glimpse of what else Mother had wanted to tell me. My entire body went cold in spite of the evening heat radiating through the window.

A deep sigh escaped. "Listen, Alexander, this is a heck of a shock. I… I have your number and you now have mine and I will, I promise you, be in touch with you at the earliest possible moment."

"Okay," the voice was very quiet. "Alright, call me soon then."

"Soon then," I echoed. "I will."

"Good bye, then" he said

"Good night" I returned.

The line was broken and I stared at the phone in my hand. This was one huge turn of events. I suddenly realized that I had not told him of Mother's death. Should I call him back? Should I wait until I pick up her remains? My Lord why had no one ever told me of this? I called for medical records and stuff to set up the cremation, why had no one said anything?

Of course, I had made that phone call to her office. Perhaps they called this young man. Perhaps that was where they expected to reach her thinking I simply did not know her home phone number. Then I realized that I probably did not have the proper number. I checked my cell against the numbers I had for her in my address book. It did match an old number that mother had told me not to use as it had been disconnected. What had she been doing all these years? My mind raced with possibilities. I thought of calling Shelly again but quickly realized that if she had known this news, she would definitely have told me long before now.

Thoughts whirled through my mind then suddenly stuck on the young man's name. Alexander. She finally got to name someone after her brother. I felt oddly jealous. Did that make this boy more important than me? Why could she not have shared this part of her with me? Where in the heck was he when I did live with her my first years in college? I kept my distance and stayed busy but I really would have noticed another person living with us. Perhaps he was actually a stepson and only called her 'mother' like I called Shelly 'Mom'. Still the last name was the same…actually the same as mine. Was my father his father? Were there secrets too awful to tell? Once again, the phone in my hand rang without warning and I jumped straight up.

"Yes, yes, hello" I stammered into the phone.

"Hello, Doctor Livingston, it is me, Tanemghurt." The familiar voice came through with static. "I have just talked with my brother who said you were still in Rabat. He said you were at the church. Did you learn anything?"

I felt breathless and foggy. With some effort I remembered the visit with the priest and realized that I did need to share some other news.

"Ah, yes, Tanemghurt," I stammered, "it is really good to hear your voice. Are you doing, okay?"

"Very much okay; you are well?" she said.

"Yes, I'm fine." I knew I would be fine…someday. I went on to share what I had learned from the priest without getting into the subject of miracles. Tanemghurt sounded a bit let down when she heard that we still did not have a name and my disclosure that there had indeed been a woman in the area was not as reassuring to her as I had expected. There was a long pause before I heard a tiny sob from the other end of the line.

"Tanemghurt, are you alright?" I questioned.

"Why, Miss Devon," the voice came softly, "why does God hide the truth from us? What have I done wrong to make this happen?"

Her question seemed unconscionable to me. A young woman was asking if she had some control over the forces of the universe. I had just barely begun to believe there was a single entity controlling said universe and yet I was being asked such questions. My mind raced to remember the poetry in the cave. 'To one who is lost, He is the way; To one who suffers pain; He is compassion'. Was I being called upon to be the compassionate one? My own life was in such turmoil now; how could I possibly fit this question into the space of this single moment.

"Tanemghurt" I heard myself saying. "I really don't believe you are responsible for any of this. I don't know a lot about your religion but I know enough to know that this is not the way they teach that your God works. Sometimes we just are not supposed to know the answers to every question, at least, not right now. The answers will come… someday… I believe."

Quiet sobs continued through the phone from miles away. I felt more than heard her voice traveling across the desert. It somehow seemed right to allow her to weep as I sat in silence. My mind drifted back to the sound of the Englishman I had just spoken to "…you have news of my mother…". He sounded so properly British; I tried to form an image of what he must look like.

"Miss Devon," Tanemghurt's soft voice broke into my thoughts. "Perhaps I must call back another time."

"Why" I was truly concerned for my friend.

"I don't know. Maybe you think I am childish." She sounded hurt.

"No" I needed to be truthful. "I can't understand your deep concern over this matter but I am not a believer in your faith, so maybe I am not the person who can help you understand it all. I can feel your concern but…"

"But you were there in the cave" Tanemghurt broke in, "you heard the words of the Ancient One, you know that I am healed. I shared so much about my people. How can you not believe?"

They were all valid questions but how could I believe in anything when the world I knew so well was being turned upside down minute to minute?

"Tanemghurt," I finally managed to respond. "I am still working through all the information. I am sorry that I cannot just accept what you find so concrete. On the other hand, because you have always been so sure of your beliefs, perhaps you are correct… at least, for you."

"What do you mean?" the small voice quivered.

"I mean, you know what you know." I had to quiet my own fears. "It works for you and the way you choose to live your life but I don't come from the same place as you. We are not identical. I just need more time to come to understand the things which you have taken half a life time to visualize. You are not the silly one, perhaps I am."

There was a long silence before the next question. "Will you be able to continue to help us?"

I knew the answer in my heart but wanted an easy way to say it. "I'm sorry, Tanemghurt. I have found other problems I have to deal with and very little of it has to do with you. I... I have to take care of some family problems in England and then I do need to get back to my job in the United States. I'm sorry."

It was all I could say but it was the complete truth without the facts.

"I understand," the little voice was so sad. "May I call you if I find out any news?"

"Of course, you may" I really wanted to stay in touch. "I will love to hear from you. You have my cell number and I have yours. When I get back to the States I will call and get your address. Okay?"

"Okay" Tanemghurt's voice seemed to lighten. A mechanical beep interrupted our words and I knew there was a call on the other line. I explained the situation and wished her well before switching to the next call.

"Hello," I questioned almost fearful of who might be on the other end. There seemed to be only silence "Hello" I barked a second time. Now I was sorry I had not checked the caller ID to see who it was.

"I'm so sorry" came the familiar English accented voice. "I was calling because I don't know what else to do."

"Alexander?"

"Yes," he returned. "Then it is true. You are Devon Livingston and we may be related."

"Well, yes." I sensed his feeling of incredulity. "At least, it would seem so. Only I can't quite figure out how this happened."

"I think I know." His voice remained calm and almost sad. "I will be going over some old journals here and I would like very much to share them with you when you have time."

"Alexander" I interrupted. "Our mother has passed away."

"I know," he answered. "I called the hotel where she always stays in Paris and they told me."

"I'm sorry I didn't tell you before." I wanted to cry now, not for me but for this person I didn't even know.

"Well," his sad voice rejoined. "It's all a bit shocking for both of us. Will you be coming to London soon?"

"Yes, I fly to Paris in the morning and finish some business about our mother, then I will be in London and I hope you will see me." I now needed to know the person behind this voice.

"I am depending upon it. You sound very nice." He was questioning but reserved.

"You sound nice, too." I replied. "Call you from Paris before I leave."

"I shall be counting on it." He spoke.

"Goodbye." I had found no familiar name for him.

"Good night." The line buzzed.

I called the airline then the hotel in Paris. I wanted to waste no time getting to meet this person who felt like my only living relative at the moment. I thought that sleep could not possibly come as I lay back on the bed still dressed in my dark grey business suit. Who knew what other surprises were in store for me or for this person I was beginning to recognize as a brother.

I awoke to the sound of the room telephone ringing. It was the desk clerk giving me a wake-up call. The taxi I had ordered for the morning had arrived. Slightly disheveled from sleep, I quickly made my way downstairs and tried not to breathe on anyone before I found a cup of coffee at the airport.

I had planned on reflecting on the state of my life through the dark night in Morocco but my body was not willing to accommodate my want. I was happy that I had checked my luggage at the hotel in Paris and brought only a light carryon that was more a large purse than a suitcase. My forearms were beginning to tingle letting me know that I had gone too long without using my medications. In my hurry to make connections I had failed to pack them and now I was being reminded that I was not completely well.

I arrived in Paris to find the same room waiting for me with all my things as well as the luggage belonging to my mother neatly placed in closets and cupboards. I had time for a shower and a change of clothes before going to meetings with police for finalization of paperwork and another meeting to pick up the ashes. It all became very quick and my business was actually completed in a day. I had anticipated a lengthy delay as I had to prove who I was or how Mother and I were related but it all seemed to fall into place.

Then, during the taxi ride back to the hotel, I noticed a signature on one of the myriads of forms I had been given. It was Alexander Livingston. Was this my little brother? Was he some legally powerful person who could make the world move at the signing of his name? He said he was only 25, so how could this possibly be a reality? Surely, I would have heard of a famous person by that name? On the other hand, I had never heard of the name at all before my conversation with Mom.

The taxi came to a halt in front of the hotel. I wandered slowly through the lobby looking now at the last places I had seen Mother. It was as if I were seeing the places for the first time. Seeing them with myself placed in them, the alcove where we sat, the elevator doors where she attempted to make her grand entrance. How much of that last night was real and how much had I imagined through my own anger and hurt? I had wanted to be able to love my mother but there was always some barrier between us.

I sat on an upholstered bench and sank into a reverie. I did the math concerning our ages, Alexander was born when I was about eight years old, the same time as the twins. I had always believed that she was in the next state, going to school and quietly avoiding me. Did this mean she was in England back then? Was this other life more like what she wanted than I was? I suddenly felt stupid and childish. Here I was, a grown woman, feeling pangs of jealousy over a situation from the long past; a situation with no answers because the only person who truly knew was now dead. I felt something drop on my hand and opened my eyes to find I was silently crying.

Suddenly, a hand covered my tears and I jumped. It was the concierge, a kindly older gentleman. He spoke softly and suggested that I might call a friend or family member. I thought how ironic it was that there was actually someone I could call. I thanked him and said I would simply retire. I took my time going up to my room and just as I arrived at the door, a bellboy came with a tray containing hot tea and a few chocolates. It was a thoughtful touch but left me feeling even more alone. I had become an object of pity and I did not like it. This must be the fate of the cowbird, a creature to be pitied.

I slept in fits and starts for the next night and day. No one called to break the silence of my room and I chose to close myself into a cocoon of sorrow and tears. A part of me felt sad that my mother was gone, as contentious as our relationship had been; she was still a person I had known. Another part of me was angry at her deception and manipulative behavior. How could she have chosen not to share a whole person with me? I had a brother, living and breathing in the world and she did not even tell me. No one I knew had ever mentioned it or intimated that it was possible.

I wandered the streets of Paris as I ran the math in my head. If Alexander was born when I was eight, that meant he was about the same age as my twin sisters. That meant that he was ten when I graduated from high school and moved off to college to live for the next three years with my mother. I know I would have noticed a ten-year-old boy in that apartment. Where was he, living with his father in England? I wondered if she had treated him the same way. No phone calls, no visits, just a hidden knowledge that somewhere out there was a person who had given birth to him. I grew angry mentally condemning her for her abandonment of yet another child.

Then the anger would subside and I would remember the words in the cave about forgiveness and reaching out. That's what I had not done most of my life. I stayed busy working and going to class. The relationships I did have were with men and they were always physical. There had been some who might have wanted more but it was as if a bell went off in my head warning me to break it off and run away.

I began to compare myself to my mother, this Alexis/Anna Ruth person I barely knew. Shelly had talked about her being a party girl and there was more than one time I came in from class to find yet another new man in the living room. Mother once told me she "enjoyed the beginnings of romance but could not bear to be shackled by the bonds of marriage". What had she actually been doing all the hours I was away at school? We ate carry out and cereal so she didn't cook and there was a cleaning lady who came in once a week so she didn't have to clean. She always talked about a research paper she was working on but I never saw or heard about any results from it. On the other hand, she had to have some sort of income because we were never really without anything. I remembered the conversation about my dad's support but that still would not have been enough to cover all the expenses. Perhaps my mother was even more devious than I suspected. Perhaps that also helped explain her extreme need to maintain a certain appearance at all times. I tried visiting several churches in the area, there are many beautiful cathedrals in Paris but still I remained cold.

I continued to wallow in my grief, allowing myself to move freely between anger and despair and shame. Yes, it was shame at who I was and who she had been. For all my anger toward her I still began to face my own demons. I began to remember the anger and jealousy I displayed toward Shelly and how I had tried to blame her for all the wrong things in my own life. I considered calling her again and apologizing but by then it was the third week of my stay in Paris and I had scheduled a flight to London.

CHAPTER 13
AN INTERLUDE

Devon had stopped once again. I looked to see great streams of tears falling onto the table top. She excused herself and dashed for the lady's room. I glanced round to see the waitress, now joined by a similarly clad woman, glaring at me as if to say I had best watch my step. No doubt she had been witness to many lover's quarrels and temper tantrums but I felt at a loss as to how to explain what had occurred. I fiddled with my empty coffee cup, finally turning it upside down and waving it in the air until the woman behind the counter came with a full pot to fill us up again.

She bent low, "Not meaning to be nosy, but is the lady all right?" Perhaps she was not glaring but only concerned.

"Why, yes" I stammered "at least I believe so. She has had quite a shock recently; death in family and all." The nameless woman nodded knowingly then smiled a little as she turned back to the counter. I could tell by the look on the other woman's face that some silent or near silent communication was going on between them. I suppose the lack of shouting or cursing had been some clue that things were simply becoming emotional rather than violent.

Devon returned, more subdued now. Her smiling, flirty attitude had disappeared to be replaced by one of solemn reflection.

"Fred," she began "what is it that causes us to stop in the middle of a busy life and try to figure out what is going on? I realize that the deaths of my mother and Mom are sort of watershed moments that called my own mortality to mind but somehow all of this was more than that." Her mood was becoming academic, a more comfortable place for me.

"How do you mean?" I asked.

"Well, the time in the cave. The words of the ancient one still haunts me." Her brow furrowed and she stared at her hands. "The things she said are somehow connected to everything, everything I have experienced and maybe will experience. I just can't seem to get a grip on it all."

"Did you ever go back and talk with the priest or study the books he gave you?"

"No," she answered "not really. I looked at a few of the chapters while I was waiting to fly on to London but after that I really never picked them up again."

Perhaps this was not a conversion story; perhaps it was the story of a quest of some other sort. My own work in anthropology touches on the spiritual beliefs of many of the different groups of people who exist in the world. Quest stories among Native North American and South American peoples spring to mind most immediately. Was she searching for something else? Was she looking less for a God and more for true self?

"Why didn't you pursue them?" I asked.

"Honestly?" she looked deeply into my eyes and a chill ran down my spine. "It was because of all that happened next. There was never time to stop and just read a book. There were moments to ponder, conversations with the family I was going to see but reading time was not available."

I knew we were about to plunge again into the story once more, but this time I moved my hand to the back of her chair. Rather than move away as she had previously, she seemed to move in to me. She leaned her head against my shoulder, sighed and began again.

CHAPTER 14
A FAMILY

The flight across the channel was horrible. Take off was delayed for over an hour and most of us on board were very anxious. It was Fall heading into winter and the storms were brewing everywhere. I had started to read one of the books from Fr. Christian during the delay but even the thought of reading during the flight felt absurd. I had called Alexander before leaving the hotel that morning but only reached his answer machine with my flight and arrival information. I thought about checking one of the other numbers Mother had given me at her work or office but then decided that this would be enough. If he could not be there to meet my plane, I was prepared to take a taxi to a hotel. Finding him could wait a day or so; after all I had waited all of my life to meet him, another day would not matter. As we pitched and rolled, I chided myself for choosing to fly. I knew that Mother always took the Euro train but until this moment never knew why.

The woman sitting next to me must have been a Christian because she kept clutching a small black book and calling on God to protect us all. I felt as though I agreed with her but I did not have the words available in my memory the way she seemed to. Then a vision came to me of the Ancient One standing in the rubble. She spoke no words but raised her hand in much the same way that Fr. Christian had each time we parted.

Suddenly the plane shuddered and we began a nearly straight nosedive toward the ocean or the ground, I did not know which. The oxygen masks dropped signaling a drop in cabin pressure and all the people around me began to reach for the life vest tucked under the seat. In all my years of Trans Atlantic travel I had never had to use the information they had so carefully disseminated. Now it was time to move and try to stay calm. The stewards were helping some with their gear and telling us to stay calm, reminding us of the drill they had worked so long to memorize. It is real, I thought, I will die here in a foreign country without ever knowing the truth about the ancient one or who my Mother really was. I bent over and held on as bumps became harder. Then we were slammed into the ground and the plane seemed to come apart at a seam just in front of me.

Next a pair of hands pulled me up at the shoulders and flicked off my seat belt. I barely had time to see the face of a tall thin young man as he lifted me over my seat mate and into the aisle. We dashed for the opening and he pulled me down on to the ground.

"Run" he shouted through the pouring rain. "Run as fast as you can."

There was crashing thunder and terrible lightning all around. The ground was more rock than dirt and we slid on the surface. I fell several times tearing the delicate skin on my forearms, only recently healed from the time in the cave. I knew I was bleeding but there was no time to stop and tend to it. Then I heard the screams of the other passengers. I pulled on my rescuers hand.

"Wait," I said "What about the others."

"Can't go back," he screamed over the roar of thunder. He pulled my aching arm and gestured toward a hollowed-out area in a sheer rock wall. It was another cave. I pulled back not wanting to enter. He pulled with greater ferocity and threw me into the cave entrance. We were not completely out of the weather but enough to feel safe from the lightning. We huddled together, gasping for air and staring at the great silver aircraft cracked open in three places as it draped across the jagged rocks. We had come down on land very near the ocean. I saw the frothy, silver waves jumping in the light of the storm flashes. The people on board were streaming away from the plane, some running, some turning back to help others from the broken craft.

"That's weird," my friend whispered "there's no fire."

"What" I questioned.

"No fire" he repeated as he began to release his hold on me, "at least not yet."

"I hope there won't be one." I offered, "Maybe all of the passengers will get out alive."

"Sure" he returned. I could feel him looking at me in the dark and I let go of his shoulder moving slightly away. "Are you hurt? I think you are bleeding."

A lightning flash revealed a young man holding his hand over his eyes as if to shield them from the light.

"It's my arms," I offered "they were kind of beat up as we came across the rocks." I knew the long explanation was not appropriate here.

He said nothing more but turned and looked toward the emergency scene before us. It had been mid-morning of a beautiful late autumn day when we left Paris but now it was nearly as dark as night although I was fairly certain it was less than three hours since we had taken off. The storm had to have come up out of nowhere. The authorities and airlines were usually so vigilant in watching for possible storms. We were far more likely to have been grounded for extra hours than to have flown into this mess.

I wondered who my young savior was and why of all the passengers on board he had chosen me. I did not remember seeing him among the other guests. Then as if he read my mind, he turned to me and offered his hand.

"Hi," he intoned as the storm seemed to subside, "my name is Alex Livingston and, correct me if I'm wrong, but aren't you, Devon?"

My heart nearly skipped a beat as my jaw dropped and I grasped his hand reflexively.

"Why, yes" I stammered "yes, I am. How did you…? I thought you were…? What?"

He began to smile slowly.

"Hi, Sis" he said curtly. His hair was dirty blonde and wavy, his face a gentle triangle ending in a pronounced cleft chin, certainly not like any member of my family. Yet his eyes were unmistakably Mother's. Cool, blue and capable of looking directly into my own eyes. He smiled sheepishly and waited as if to see what I might do next.

"Good Lord," I spoke, "you have her eyes."

"I could have picked you out of a line up, you know." He giggled.

"Do you think there are any more of us?" My mind seemed a jumble of questions and quirky observations.

"Don't know yet, don't know if I want to find out?" Alexander continued to stare at me and I could not tear myself away from him. Suddenly I became aware of a bright steady glow; the aircraft was beginning to burn. Sirens began to wail off in the distance as if there were emergency vehicles coming to our rescue. Perhaps there was a town or village nearby where people had heard the noise from the crash. Just as quickly as the storm had come up, it began to subside and move away. The sun began to glow behind scattering clouds.

"C'mon" said Alexander tugging at my arm which now seemed to ache even more. "We better get back down there so the rescue people can look at your injuries."

I followed him back down a thin sandy path between the boulders. As we approached, we noticed that the crew had begun to fight the fire with small extinguishers. It seemed to be contained in the cabin at the front of the plane. We joined a small group of passengers at the edge of the sand and waited. Fortunately, I seemed to have been the most badly damaged of all in my group. My upper left arm was broken as well as the tears and bruises to my skin. I was covered in blood so I was wrapped in a warm blanket and whisked away to the village hospital. In the confusion, I lost sight of Alexander.

Once again there were bandages and pain killers. My new brother had actually obtained a ride with one of the local officials and followed me to the hospital. Except to find a place to stay and retrieve our belongings from the airlines, he never left my side. I was retained in the hospital for over three weeks fighting a new infection in my skin. I was in and out of consciousness in the beginning but eventually I reclaimed my senses and was able to communicate.

The days of physical therapy and replacing bandages were long and grueling but Alexander became the happy part of each day. He was an excellent story teller and entertained me with the story of his life as he avoided my gaze by staring off into the English countryside.

CHAPTER 15
ALEXANDER'S STORY

My father's name is Alexander so the family tends to call me Alex or Lex, I am his only son but have grown up with lots of cousins. Dad is a missionary with the Episcopal Church and tends to travel well over half of the time preaching and teaching in all the continents of this world. I have actually been raised by my grandparents and two maiden aunts. Had it not been for Granddad, I suppose I might have been the only boy in my home. It certainly was not a bad life at all. My Grandparents are quite wealthy; some lands passed down from the early ages have provided them with income along with thoughtful investments in areas of financial growth. In many ways I was very spoiled and favored, the reason being that I had been abandoned by Mother and therefore was deserving of extra special care.

The story had always been told that I had come to life during one of my father's darker moments while he was at college abroad. He took some of his seminary studies in America, so that; I now suppose, is where he met our mother. He never talks about it and I had always assumed that he was simply ashamed of his conduct but in the end, it is of little matter, at least to me. According to my birth records I was born in England in a women's shelter and given up for adoption on the day of that birth. Some family member or possibly even my father heard of the transaction and came swooping in to rescue me from whatever horrible fate lay in store for me. The odd thing is that my name was never changed to my father's family name of Hudson. I was given our mother's surname of Livingston and it has never changed. As a schoolboy I often dreamed of changing it but any time I broached the subject, Father would turn away and speak of something else.

As I say, my childhood was not bad or deprived; just very lonely. Proper school children in England are still often sent away at a young age to be taught and that is exactly what happened for me. I lived large portions of each year after the age of ten at boarding school. Truthfully, home with grandparents and cousins was more raucous but still very lonely. I believe that I was closer to a couple of my schoolmates in those growing years than I was to family members.

I was schooled with the intention that I might follow my father into mission work but I knew rather early on that I found no value in that. The Christian schools I attended were good but I learned quickly to follow along and hide my true feelings when in the presence of any teacher or head master. In that manner I managed to learn quite a few facts about Christianity without having to actually be involved in the emotional parts of it all.

I worked very hard and obtained quite respectable marks so I was granted entry into studies at Oxford. I chose psychology and have pursued that degree with diligence. I have just this year completed my studies and been accepted into a doctoral program which allows me to conduct research and teach.

I actually met our mother for the first time when I was new at university about six years ago. I had been invited to a party at the home of one of our professors; I was being shown off as the next up and coming bright star in our school. Our regally dressed mother approached and introduced herself. I remember that she seemed to hesitate as if waiting for me to somehow recall exactly who she was in relation to me. Knowing her now, I see that this is just her way. If she knows a fact, she assumes all those in her circle have that same knowledge. If the fact concerns her, then all the more reason to assume that knowledge is general.

She continued to stare at me throughout the evening, or at least that is how it felt. Not a continual stare but I became more and more uncomfortable, as if she were watching my every move. Finally at the end of the occasion I approached her by commenting on our identical surname. That it seems was just the opening she required. She pulled me off into a small hallway and told me point blank that she was my mother. She pressed a card into my hand and said that if I wished, I might call her and we could meet to share the details.

Of course, I did call her. How could I not. I believed she had the answer to so many questions I had been hiding in my heart. Her version was rather different than the one I had grown up with, of course. She had indeed met Father at school but had traveled with him to England hoping to be allowed to meet his parents and be welcomed into the family. This did not happen; in fact, they were quite adamant that Father give up any relationship with her and continue his studies. If he were to search for a wife, she should be a proper English girl from a good family and not a foreigner. Truth was, my grandparents never even met her and their harsh feelings toward her were based solely on their mistrust of people from other backgrounds.

Paradoxically, this is always the way they were. 'Foreign folk' were fine if they were non-Christian, back-water, uneducated needy folk for whom they could feel pity. They hated Americans because they were actually successful. Although to this day, I don't believe they think that American are Christians. Mother may have been one to enhance the truth from time to time, but for this theory about my Grandparents, she was spot on.

Anyway, this woman standing before me, telling me this tale seemed as if she were relating the plot to some play or mini drama. Father had left her at a hostel in London saying he would come back for her as soon as he had properly prepared his parents to meet her. Yet, it seems she was not without resources even in a distant land so while waiting to see if she would be given an audience with her intended in-laws; she obtained a position with a research firm here in London. She began work immediately and did not hear from Father for nearly ten days, when she did it was a hurried phone call from the airport saying he was leaving on assignment with the Church and he would ring her up on his return in six months. Well, as the classic story goes, a week later she found she was 'with child' and felt there was nothing to do but wait until the fated phone call. Of course, she managed to move on to a small flat near her work and could not find a way to leave a new number for Father to reach her. It was all terribly dramatic and, as we both know, no one could pull off melodrama better than Mother.

I wavered back and forth for several days after the meeting about seeing her again. Not that I doubted her but I am by nature rather suspicious of melodrama; could not quite figure out what she could possibly want from me. Eventually I did phone her up and we met again at a little tea shop near campus. These meetings went on for about a month. Every few days I would find time in my schedule to fit in a meet and she would oblige. It was not until the end of term that I found out her real request.

Economy had gone a bit off and she had been put on part time at her work. The result of course was that she could no longer afford to stay in her home and wanted my help. Well, I was working as well as having a stipend for school from family so it was obvious that I should take a large flat and we would begin to share a space. It was awkward at first, I having been used to living in my own quarters at home and in a bachelor flat at school but we adjusted. I went home for a week here or there to keep my grandparents happy but never told them about our arrangement or about my having met her. Things went on quite well until end of my final year when graduation was upon me and my grandfather showed up at the school to 'help me' with arrangements.

He had gone to the rooms where my classmates all lived and the place, they had been sending my mail to for the last months and, of course my friends told him I had moved. I had failed to swear them to secrecy never dreaming that Granddad might do such a thing. Of course, he went straight away to the flat I shared with Mother; I was still in class and was totally unaware until my friend, Jason sent me a text. Mother was home so you can well imagine what ensued. It was quite funny really. Granddad had never met Mother so when this woman opened the door, he at first assumed that I had taken up with some older woman. He asked for me and was told I was in class. Mother, having never met Granddad invited him in to wait for my imminent arrival. Once inside, Grandfather decided that perhaps I had become much wealthier than he had imagined and had hired a maid or cleaning woman to tidy up as Mother was dressed so casually.

Entrance into the apartment showed him that I did indeed live there as my personal photos and knick-knacks could be seen about the place. When Mother placed herself in a suitable chair after making tea for the both of them, he again pursued the thought that I was living with this woman in an unacceptable manner. Grandfather became increasingly confused as Mother prattled on about how well I was doing in school and how proud she was of me. Grandfather listened, incredulous then rose from his chair to begin to question her seemingly intimate knowledge of his grandson.

About this time, I reached the doorway of my rooms and could do little more than smile awkwardly. There were halting introductions for me to make and a very uncomfortable silence hung over the space. I am sure each one was thinking of the hateful things each had stated about the other. For my part I felt quite sheepish knowing I had kept certain information from each one. Mother, of course, was the first to break the silence.

"Alexander, my son," she spoke emphasizing each word. "Mother is feeling very perplexed at the moment. Mightn't we be introduced?"

"Certainly," I sputtered. "Mrs. Livingston; Sir Gregory Hudson, my grandfather, Grandfather this is my mother." Granddad cleared his throat and sank heavily into the chair. Never once had he suspected that this woman with the proper English accent could possibly have been my American mother. He kept shaking his head as if to clear away his thoughts.

"Grandfather," I felt he deserved an explanation first. "This is my natural mother, Miss Alexis Livingston. She was born in America but has been working and living here in England for quite some time. Grandfather nodded in her direction and muttered a greeting appropriate for a gentleman. "Mother," I continued, "this is my grandfather, Sir Gregory Alexander Hudson, and Earl of Braithwaite." At the mention of the title Mother's eyes widened considerably as she attempted a small seated bow.

"I had no idea," she sputtered. "Alexander never told me…"

Grandfather broke in. "Obviously, my son failed to tell me many things some years ago, for that I apologize. As for you young man, we shall speak of this at another time." He rose as if to leave.

"Grandfather, please," I interjected, "might we not be able to discuss some pertinent information? While I realize that I have been less than forthcoming in some areas…well, many areas; I am rather certain that explanations are warranted and I might say necessary at this time."

"Oh, your Grace, your Lordship," Mother began to bumble in ways that even I had never expected. Her proper English accent began to fall away. "If I had known…I'm so sorry but I…Oh, I just had never heard that you were and that this son of mine then might be…"

"Mother!" I interjected as loudly as possible before she went any further on the subject. "Mother, please… before you go down that path you must remember exactly who I am. You were there for the birth and unless you have some hidden papers to prove otherwise, I don't believe you and Father were wed then or ever." I was trying to be polite but any English schoolboy learns early on about the aristocracy and entitlement. How could she have pretended to be a part of that society and not known? In the meantime, Grandfather had turned an absolutely brilliant shade of red as his anger visibly rose.

"My good woman," he began in a whisper, his voice rising in tone and tenor with each word. "If you have any notion that this young man has any place in proper aristocratic society you are mistaken. We have taken him into our home and loved and cared for him for all of his natural life without one word from you but, a bastard he is and a bastard he shall remain. I hold you and you alone responsible for that. If you have ounce of decency in your body; you will remove yourself from these premises at once and allow young Alex to get on with his life. As far as my family and I are concerned you have only done two redeemable things in your life. The first was to give life to this precious boy and the second was to leave him alone once your services were no longer required." Shoving his hat on his head, Grandfather strode across the room and jerked open the door. "Good day!" He shouted into the room as the door slammed shut.

Mother immediately dissolved into one of the finest performances of her life. Alternately planning revenge and then sobbing uncontrollably into her linen hanky. I let her carry on for nearly half an hour until a neighbor timidly knocked to see if she might be of some assistance. I told her no but was careful to let her see that mother was quite well aside from being upset.

Needless to say, I did follow Granddad's advice and helped Mother find another flat to herself. She had been able to find temporary employment at a bookstore in Oxford so she could afford some of her care on her own. I had to supplement that but as I had a good job at a research center, I was never again dependent on my family for living expenses.

During the course of the latest installment, I had taken the liberty of resting my cheek near the top of Devon's head. This allowed me to smell her sunny, golden hair and slowly place my hand over both of hers resting atop the table. I was not ready for the moment to end but my little storyteller jumped and ended abruptly.

"Yes." She said as my eyes focused on the waitress standing before us.

"Listen, you two," she spoke in an even tone. "This ain't no lover's lane. I got my early breakfast crown on the way and they don't need to see no pair of love birds at this ungodly hour. You either order up or hit the road."

"I beg you pardon," Devon began, "we are not doing anything…"

"I know, "the waitress broke in as she began clearing away our cups, "you had a death in the family. Well, ain't we all. Sorry for your loss but I need this table for the paying customers."

I wrapped my arm around Devon's waist and lifted her to her feet before she could draw breath and begin her rebuttal. "Thank you for your odd sense of hospitality." I said, tossing a bill on the table as I glared at the woman. It was obvious we would find another place to continue.

Once outside we could see that it was nearing morning. The sun would not arrive for another hour but the full gorgeous moon was drifting just above the horizon getting ready to set. The air was much cooler. I removed my jacket and placed it around her shoulders before she slipped into the car. She looked up at me with those luminous blue eyes and I could not resist. I kissed her tenderly, softly then once more as if to assure myself that her lips were as lovely as they seemed.

"Oh, Freddy," she breathed and closed her eyes, "let's just go somewhere, I can't stand to be alone right now."

Could she possibly have thought that I wanted to leave her now? Even the way she called me Freddy didn't seem so awful anymore. We got into the car and headed back toward town still enjoying the wind in our hair. Devon was huddled into my coat and I took the liberty of reaching for her hand. She did not pull away. The radio was still on with some later Beatles hits rolling out into the morning air.

Driving along I thought about her story again. It still had all the earmarks of a conversion story but that was not the way she was acting. There had been only the relating of this period in her life; no mention of miracles for herself so far. Now she had let me kiss her and the stories of her promiscuous past came to mind. I wondered how I fit into the scheme of her thinking. Maybe she wasn't really thinking anymore; perhaps she was so hurt and wounded by all that had happened that she was clinging to me for emotional support.

"That's the way they do it you know," a little voice in my head spoke. I had heard this voice before when I was going through my divorce from Helen. "They put you in a position where you begin to believe that they need you and then they toss you around like a rag doll." My little voice was very anti-woman having been present each time my heart was broken. I knew I could not control how this time with Devon would evolve but she was so captivating. This is always how men get in trouble. I knew I was tired because the thoughts continued to roll around in my mind. So many open-ended questions; so few answers that I could nail down. Instinctively I headed straight for my own apartment.

Devon turned off the radio and indicated that she was ready to continue her story. I rolled to the side of the road and put the top up. Things would not be silent but at least we would be able to hear one another.   So, she continued.

By the time we were ready to leave the hospital in England, it was nearly Christmas. Alex invited me to come and spend the rest of my recuperation time with him at his two-bedroom townhouse in London. I was leery but as there were few other options, I decided to take him up on the offer. My position at my university was now considered vacant and any planned spring classes either cancelled or reassigned to another professor. I could have flown home but I wanted to stay close to this family I was just beginning to know.

The ride across England on the train was cozy and uneventful. A lovely snow had fallen blanketing the countryside in mounds of white. The train rattled quietly and seemed to help my aching arms, bandaged and still in a sling; feel better as we sat across from one another in a little compartment.

The main thing that I learned about my little brother was that he was very contemplative. I really don't think I had ever met anyone who kept to himself as much as he did. In the hospital he had been cheerful and full of stories about his childhood and the few trips he had taken with his father; but once we boarded the train a grey silence seemed to envelope him. He was bright and rather handsome in his very quiet way but it was his eyes that mesmerized me. They were bright sky blue and more piercing than Mother's, if that was even possible.

I was finally able to muster the courage to ask Alexander why he was on the flight from Paris the day we crashed. I had wondered about that off and on in the hospital but the drugs and therapies always kept questions from forming while he was in the room. Of course, I had spent a good deal of time telling him about my adventures in Africa and my childhood, too.

"Well, it's simple really," he said with an impish grin, "I could no longer wait to see you. I had flown to Paris two days before and found your hotel. A simple maneuver as it was the same one where Mother always stayed. I was going to surprise you there but just couldn't do it. I got hold of one of the staff who was willing to tell me your flight schedule. I had planned on flying with you and if I could not speak to you on the flight, I would still be there to meet you at the airport."

"You are a very sneaky little brother." I teased. I envisioned him peeking out from behind the columns in the lobby observing me as I walked.

"And you, my dear, are a very adventurous big sister." His voice softened as he appeared to consider us. "I am also rather shy, not a good quality in a Doctoral candidate. We are an odd little family."

I knew he was including our mother. "Yes," I added, "my step mother says she was like a cowbird. That's a bird that lays its egg in other bird's nests and then abandons it."

"Good analogy" he said. "Unfortunately, she seemed to show up again for both of us."

"Alex," I questioned, "where do you think she was during all the years that are unaccounted for? I actually only lived with or near her for about six- or seven-years total."

"Even less for me," he added. "I had only the last four years with her. Still during that time, I may have captured some inking of how she managed. There are diaries I found in her things in her Oxford flat. When she became ill, I was given unlimited access to all her belongings."

"Your talent for sleuthing" I noted, "must be something you developed over time." Alex's grin was infectious. I suddenly envisioned my new little brother as a ladies' man.

"Well, one cannot live where I have been without building a defense." His eyes again became withdrawn. He said so much with those eyes. "Mother always talked of parties and evenings with royal company. In all the time we were together I never once saw any of that happen. She lived a very solitary life and entertained only at home. I believe that she lived off her associations."

"You mean she was not a research scientist?" I felt a rock hit my chest.

"In the years that I was associated with her I never knew of any such work that she did at any institute in England." Hi eyes became dark and perhaps a bit angry. "The position she obtained shortly after moving in with me was one that could have been held by a first-year student. The gentleman she worked for was more than just her employer."

"But she was so old." The words burst from my mouth almost unbidden.

Alex shrugged and smiled. "Even old people need a little fun in their lives."

We both giggled as the announcement came that we had arrived at our destination. The conversation would be halted as we disembarked, gathered our luggage and found a taxi to take us to our winter home. The bulk of the items, mostly Mother's belongings, would arrive later for us to pore over and catalog as necessary or throw away.

The apartment Alex brought me into was very neat and tidy. Most of the English people I knew at home were less than diligent about housekeeping. Obviously, someone in this home had a different slant on the way things should be kept. I wondered if it was my little brother or if he simply hired help the way Mother did.

CHAPTER 16
FINDING A CENTER

As I pulled into my assigned parking space and killed the motor it dawned on me that I had not asked if this might be a place she would want to go. I looked over and noticed that her eyes were closed as if asleep. I watched the rise and fall of her breathing and leaned closer wondering if I should speak or simply kiss her again.

Her eyes popped open and a small grin began to play around her mouth. I returned her smile and moved my face within inches of her own. I am not by any standard a romantic but somehow this moment was beyond my personal impression of me and I was leading with emotion. I knew I would not kiss her.

"I forgot to ask before you drifted off." I said as simply as possible. "Would you like to come to my place for a while? It's not as tidy as your brothers flat and I do share it with a large yellow striped cat but it is indoors and there are no waitresses."

She giggled softly. "I think I would like that." She sat upright still smiling and handed me my jacket. We exited the car and fell into step as she allowed me to take her hand once more. We entered the building in silence and climbed the single stairway to my door. It unlocked easily and I thought again of trying to kiss her but she moved quickly past me and I reached to turn on the light; an empty move at best as it was just past sunrise and the room was lit from outside.

I realized that my description of my apartment as less than tidy was embarrassingly correct. Stacks of books and papers seemed to cover most of the flat surfaces and a pair of trousers was draped across the back of one chair. The cat had taken up residence in the center of the sofa between a stack of ungraded papers and a basket of clean laundry. I was surprisingly grateful that the laundry was clean.

"Oh," Devon cooed, "what a pretty cat. What's his name? May I pet him?"

"Well," I responded hanging my jacket in the closet, "her name is Cecily and I am really not sure. She can be nice when she wants to be but she did nip at the neighbor boy once. She belongs to my mother who was kind enough to wire me last week and let me know that she had left with my father on a cruise and would I be so kind as to care for their pet. My parents are a bit of a handful I'm afraid."

Cecily greeted her name with a meow and offered to vacate the sofa rather than deal with a new person in the room. It was just as well as far as I was concerned. I tossed the laundry basket in the closet, grabbed my trousers off the chair and motioned for Devan to take the place of the cat after I brushed quickly at the cushion.

"May I offer you a cup of coffee," I suddenly remembered my manners. "I can guarantee it will be better than that stuff we tried to drink at the café."

"Now that was terrible." Devon answered. She sat down and leaned back as I headed for the kitchen. "You know, Fred, I'm really tired. Maybe I should just go home."

"Well," my mind began to scramble for reasons to keep her here. "I can certainly understand that but I don't think you are really at the end of your story and this will just be instant coffee… we can be wide awake in no time."

Silence drifted from the living room as I placed the kettle on to boil. I thought about it for a moment and pulled two cups from the cupboard, filled them with water, and stuck them in the microwave. "Devon," I called softly. The timer went off as I was laying our spoons and instant coffee on a tray. I snatched the cups from the microwave and headed for my guest.

"Devon" I repeated, hoping she had no nodded off again. "I'm not sure how you like it… sugar or milk or both?

As I entered Devon seemed to be leaned forward with her hands clasped in front of her. I placed the tray gently on an open space near her and joined her on the couch.

"Are you okay?" I questioned softly.

"Sure," she said looking up. "Just thinking about the words of the Ancient One again. Sometimes they really come back to haunt me." She stared at the tray of coffee things for a moment before continuing. "Fred, do you think there is a God? I mean one that really is totally involved in human beings' lives?"

"I don't know," I mused as I took a seat next to her. "There are certainly a large number of people who seem to think so and, if memory serves me correctly, this idea has gone on for several thousands of years through many different groups of human beings. But if there is this God then why are we so awful to one another, especially the one claim to be members of the religions who worship this God?"

"Well," she interjected, "I am no expert on religion of any kind; but I don't think one has that much to do with the other."

"How do you mean?"

"Well," she reasoned, "expecting perfect behavior from human beings who hold a certain belief system seems somehow ludicrous. Believing in a creator filled with unconditional love would not guarantee that we will know how to act in that same unconditional manner. History, as far as I can tell, indicates that all of life is and was and will be a learning process. Each generation has to figure things out and add some new knowledge to that data base we call life experience."

"Hmm", I interjected. "Does that mean you believe in a common knowledge base used by our spiritual senses? A sort of universal mind?"

I decided to remove the stack of papers and books from her side and replace them with two overstuffed sofa pillows. Somewhere in the back of my mind I was remembering our positions at the lounge and I was hoping for a repeat performance as well as thinking through her statements.

"Well," she explained, "I don't think I can say that, but there is something going on cosmologically that can't be easily explained. I attended several lectures some years ago that dealt with the subject of astrophysics and cosmology. There were very good speakers at some of them but I can't say I came away with conclusions. There was one line from the Ancient One when she said 'each generation must seek its own questions'. "

Devon leaned back on the pillows just as I had hoped. "I don't know, Freddy," she stifled a yawn. "You didn't hear her in the cave… we, you couldn't have really…you were here and not there so…she was just so mysterious and yet not really. There was this sense… this aura of something…" Her eyes closed with a sigh. Had I bored her to sleep?

Watching Devon dozing I tried to envision all the scenes she had shared with me up to this point. Once again, I was drawn to my own personal quest for that elusive connection. Was I looking for a person who would complement myself or was there really a human need to bond with a creator being: Perhaps I was just tired and maybe my head hurt.

I awoke to the sound of the cat purring in my ear. She had climbed across the top of the sofa and was sitting exactly opposite my ear; it was a part of her morning wakeup routine. I opened my eyes to find Devon softly snoring at the other end of the couch, sunlight streaming in from all sides. It was obviously late into the morning if not actually afternoon. Devon stirred slightly as I stood so I covered her with a small quilt and headed into the kitchen to take care of the cat. The tea kettle was still cooking on the stovetop, the water completely boiled away.

I muttered to the cat a bit as I fed her then began to prepare a real cup of coffee. This was not the time for instant anything. As I pushed the button to begin the brew cycle, I heard a shuffle behind me and looked to see Devon propped against the kitchen door frame wrapped in the quilt.

"Fred," she drawled, "I really think I need to go home now. I mean I really like being with you but I think we both need some sleep." I walked over and wrapped my arms around her.

"I agree." I said, kissing the top of her head. She hugged me back and we began to rock from side to side slightly. She had removed her shoes and her make-up was worn away. She lifted her chin and I kissed her lips and she kissed me back. I stroked her cheek with my fingertips.

"I'm just going to use your… you know? She pointed in the direction of the bathroom. I nodded and turned to get the coffee things together. This was not the lusty sort of feeling I often got when dealing with women up close; this was softer and quiet somehow. I found two Styrofoam cups in my cabinet left over from some ancient gathering and poured them full. Devon had returned to put her shoes on by the time I reached the living room again and handed one of the cups to her.

"Sugar is still there if you like." I pointed to our cups from earlier. "I know you are right about needing sleep and I can take you home or back to your car if you are still on campus."

"Oh, home would be fine." She was sleepy but a bit more alert. "I walked over yesterday so my car is still at the apartment." She dropped in sugar, tasted, and then added one more. Even with the worn away make-up she looked absolutely beautiful standing there in the sunlight.

"So, tell me," I said as we began to walk out, "how did things go with you and your brother. We sort of ended when you reached London before Christmas. I think you have about four months or so to fill in here."

"You mean you still want to hear about this?" she queried.

"I told you" I insisted, "I'm in this to the end. If we're going to write this down, we can hardly end it with a tidy flat in England and you magically appearing in America…alone…four months later, now, can we?"

"No," she answered, "that would be more like my mother's life."

Driving across town her story continued.

CHAPTER 17
HER STORY CONTINUES

We were in London, my new brother and me, at Christmas time in a nice two story, two-bedroom apartment. It was very tastefully decorated in the spare 1970's style so popular in recent years. All rust and tan with light wood accents, there was even a hint of avocado appliances in the kitchen.

We stayed in mostly, reading tons of papers that belonged to our mother gathered from a large steamer trunk Alex had pulled from her room. She really was not a research scientist but she did write like one. A talent she likely developed while studying during her graduate school days. She kept diaries of almost every day of her life. I read her life backwards beginning with the weeks of illness before I met her in Paris and continuing all the way back to her days in college when she first met my dad.

Alex was basically right; our mother lived off the kindness of strangers for big portions of her life. She had inheritances from time to time and tried to invest it but she did not seem to be particularly gifted in making financial decisions. She was very candid about everything often sharing with her diary how she would get money or things from a gentleman without falling into a permanent marital arrangement. She was never married to anyone but my dad and seemed to feel that being single was a perfect way of life for her.

Sadly, for Alex, we found that she had received an extremely large amount of money in exchange for him at birth. Her story of being stranded was a complete fabrication and her 'surprise' at learning of his grandfather's title was just one more act in her life-drama. His father had met her at my university and she had followed him back to England without his realizing it. Worse still she had intentionally gotten pregnant to try and trap his family into a lifelong support arrangement. She had not counted on Alexander's parents' willingness to accept the baby and raise him as if he were their own. She seemed shocked whenever she found that not everyone thought as she did. The only part that was true was that this Grandparents had never wanted to meet her.

I, on the other hand, was not planned but had arrived before mother began her scheming ways in earnest. She was still a young woman trying to live according to the moral standards set by her parents and community. She did support Dad through school and tried to be a good wife and mother; but it all became too much for her. Going through the divorce was very upsetting according to the journals and I could sense a growing anger as she went through the months of becoming a single parent. Her frustration at this way of life was very apparent.

Oddly, her turning me over to Dad didn't seem to have the impact I was expecting. It was a one- line entry. 'Sent Devon to Kansas, maybe now I'll get some much-needed rest.' The entries following were all about classes and men she met. I felt a twinge of sadness but then remembered that this was the mother I had come to know and decided the emotional expense was too great. I decided I would be wasting my time and energy being angry or even upset.

While we were busy reading and growing in our knowledge of the woman who had given us life, I began to dream of the Ancient One and hear again the words she had shared in the cave. Almost every night I would wake up, covered in sweat and breathing heavily following the dream. I would be in the cave again only this time it would be full of light rather than darkness. The small black woman with the white, wispy hair and large dark eyes was sitting in a lotus position on a large stone slightly above me. The voice she spoke in was Tanemghurt's, the words identical to what I heard all those months before. Lessons on salvation and forgiveness poured out and seemed to fill the air with extra brilliant drops of light like snowflakes falling in sunshine. I felt warm and comforted as I dreamed but then I would wake up with a sense of great loneliness wrapped around me. Several nights I tossed and turned for hours trying to fall back to sleep. Eventually, I wrote down the poems the Ancient One had shared with me in the cave.

In the cold early morning hours, I would lie awake and try to talk to this God that seemed so important to the people I had met in the North African desert. I did not have words like the prayers they said in the Mass so I just tried to talk in my own voice and in my own way. It was awkward at first but after a few tries I began to feel as if someone somewhere actually heard me. It was odd really, not like a voice or anything but just a knowing in my heart that they or he knew how I felt.

During this same time, I began to notice that Alex was becoming even more silent and withdrawn. The grey cloud that I had noticed on the train seemed to grow and deepen. I felt as if he were drifting away from me and turning in on himself. I tried to find ways to share my dreams and the words of hope with him but the time always seemed wrong or he would change the subject.? Days loomed ahead of us; I entered the living room to find Alex sitting on the sofa with his back to the room, staring out the window and crying quietly. He made no sound but his shoulders were shaking as tears streamed down his cheeks.

"Alex?" I called softly as I walked to sit behind him. "Are you okay?"

He turned further away from me and began to wipe his eyes on his sleeve.

"Alex," I touched his shoulder but he moved away again.

I thought about just leaving him alone but then he made a groaning sound and began to speak in a raspy whisper.

"Why'd she do it, Devon?" he sobbed. "Why did she treat us like dirt — like some piece of furniture to be bargained with?" With each word he became more agitated. "why'd she leave these damn diaries for us to learn about it?" He turned and looked deeply into my eyes. "It's not fair. It's not fair to treat someone like that but it's even worse to admit it and put it in writing for the whole world to see."

Alex lurched forward and fell into my lap sobbing like a small child. "Why aren't you angry, Devon? Is it because you're not a bastard?" He spoke the last word with extra vehemence. "I'm angry. I hated being called that at school but I always knew they were telling the truth. I hated it and now I hate her."

"A part of me is angry, Alex." I spoke softly. The sling prevented me from wrapping my arms around him but I tried to gently pat his back. "I'm not pleased with her but there is something in me that hopes to forgive her."

"What?" he raised his head and looked into my eyes.

"I know how you feel, I do," I tried to explain. "I feel the same way but I keep remembering the woman in the cave and how she taught about forgiveness. Maybe it isn't the right time for you to say that but you're a psychologist; you know what anger can do to a person. How it gets inside and sort of twists you around until you can barely recognize yourself."

"Oh God, Devon," he screamed at me as he rose to his feet. "Don't ever do that to me; don't use my profession to tell me how I ought to feel or how it will make things all better. I hate you. I hate her and now I hate you too." Alex stormed to the door and grabbed his overcoat from a hook.

As he wrenched the door open, I managed to say, "Where are you going?"

"To hell," he screamed and slammed the door.

I sat there the rest of the day watching the snow turn into rain as the temperature rose slightly outside. It was two days until Christmas and there would be no celebration, no party, no feeling of joy in this home. We had called the few relatives we could reach while still at the hospital and informed them of Mother's death so we were not really expected to be anywhere for the holidays. Alex had been invited to a New Year's gathering at his Grandparents home and he let them know that he would be bringing a 'distant' relative if he attended at all. I don't think his family was pleased. He thought they suspected that the relationship would be on his mother's side.

We decided we would not exchange gifts as we felt we hardly knew one another and it was a bit difficult for me to shop with my arm still in a sling. We found a box of colored pencils and created cards for each other and Alex purchased a tiny potted tree during one of his shopping trips earlier in the week. Christmas in England would be different for me only in location.

After Dad and my sisters died, Shelley tried to have a celebration but it always felt so hollow that I would spend most of the day in my room reading and listening to music. Once I left for college the whole day was up to me so I usually chose to be somewhere else. I joined study groups and took on assignments that would take me away from festivities. It gave me a sense of control to see myself as a person more willing to work than party but I always resented those who had some special place to go. I survived most holidays by pretending they were not important to me.

I decided to make this time alone my own special retreat and hope for the best for Alex. I had no idea where or how to look for him. This was his city; I had only been here once or twice as a stopover on my way to some other destination. I thought about a lot of those destinations, the years of traveling and the people I encountered along the way. Maybe Mom was right again; somewhere in the middle of our lives we all sort of stop and consider where we have been and where we might be going. Perhaps this was my time for reviewing. I tried calling Shelley, my stepmother, but the call went straight to voice mail. I left a short wish for a Merry Christmas for her and decided she must be at Church or a neighbor's house.

One day I tried to write down the names of all the people I had been on trips and assignments with over the years. I had been thinking of Tanemghurt and her family, their close associations and how they depended upon one another for emotional support. I intended to look at those people to whom I was not related, that I relied upon for that same sort of support, since my physical family seemed so distant or absent. When I had completed it to the best of my memory, I saw that most of my companions had been men. I had never thought of this as a calculated choice on my part until now. They were not close and I did not rely on them for much of anything.

That got me thinking about my relationship status. I could not help comparing myself to the new perspective I reached concerning my mother. I had always compared myself to Mom, my Shelley, and felt embarrassed. Along with the physical care and concern I had received from Dad and Mom, there was a moral code that they tried to instill in all three of us girls. As far as I knew she had only ever been married to my dad and she had loved no other men. I, on the other hand, had taken a lover on each trip. It was never difficult; most men seemed so gullible to me. I know how to attract men but I don't think I really make friends with them. Perhaps this was the same way mother, Ms. Anna Ruth alias Alexis, had felt.

I re-read some pages of her diaries that covered years when she was not burdened with children and found them filled with references to emotional schemes she undertook just to see if she still had the ability to 'attract and capture' as she wrote in one instance. It sounded so cold, so calculated, so devious. I didn't remember feeling as if I were acting in that way. But what if I was? If I saw my mother as…a…a whore what did that make me: On the other hand, she seemed to use sex but never wrote about enjoying it and I… well, I was usually only in it for the fun. What did all this say about the way we thought of other people? Did either one of us ever think of anyone but ourselves?

I began to cry without really knowing why. There could not possibly be this great benevolent God if this was the way people treated one another. Wouldn't a God this good make everything right for those who loved him? Maybe the key to this lay in membership in an organized religion. Mother never professed and such belief but Shelly had related that dad held onto a belief in a God, even though he refused to join officially. Maybe Shelly went to a church somewhere and just didn't tell anyone back then. Maybe none of it mattered and we were really all just the product of our genetic makeup. Perhaps we could each only be slightly different than the people we came from. Perhaps there was no God and words in the cave were all a cruel joke. That night the dreams stopped.

I had a doctor's appointment three days after Christmas where I was finally relieved of my sling and given instructions for self-maintenance of my skin condition. This was the way I preferred things. The less time I spent with medical people, the better I liked it. The trip to the hospital also gave me an opportunity to walk a few streets in the neighborhood where Alex lived. It was not the oldest part of London but certainly something built after World War II. It was a lot of brick-and-mortar homes or maybe apartments. The streets were very clean and evidence of the past holiday still remained on front doors in the form of wreaths. It was cold and blustery the day I chose to walk so I did not stay out long.

Alex stayed away for over three weeks giving me ample time to consider my life as well as get past the holidays. I was sitting in my usual spot at the window sipping tea one morning when the door slowly opened and he appeared wearing the same clothes he had on when he stormed out. I walked calmly from the sofa and gave him a quick hug which he did not return. He was clean but smelled a bit of the street and cigar smoke. He placed his coat neatly on the hook next to the door and turned to me with a sheepish grin.

"Good morning, sir." I said not wanting to sound upset.

"Morning," he replied, "mind if I tidy up a bit before we talk?"

I grinned hoping to show that all was forgiven. "Of course," I said, "I'll just be right here."

I prepared a pot of tea and brought it in for us to share. I heard the shower stop and waited, wondering where on earth Alex had been for so long. I knew him well enough by now to know I had better not push but let him answer my questions as he chose. He entered the room in fresh clothing, his hair still wet and shining, and came to sit across from me on the couch.

"Oh," he said, glancing at the two teacups on the tray, "this won't be quite enough. I have asked a guest to join us." He rose and moved quickly into the kitchen.

"Anyone I should know?" I asked.

"No, I doubt it." Alex entered and sat again. "He is an old friend of my Father's, a missionary pal; they spent a good deal of time together in Africa. He's really a nice fellow and he may be able to help us with some of your questions about those Catholic Berbers you had some dealings with."

"Really?" I was shocked. All his anger at our mother seemed to have disappeared; the entire emphasis changed, "Alex, where the heck have you been for three weeks?" I questioned.

He smiled and poured his tea.

"Well, if you must know" he began as he rose from his seat to pace, teacup in hand, "I went on a bender when I left here. A real pub crawl that lasted for six days; drank until my money ran out then fell asleep in a flop house in some seedy part of the inner city. My Dad friend found me there and took me to his place to dry out."

"Okay," I answered evenly. I was not his mother or his wife so I felt it would be inappropriate to pass any kind of judgement on his life. He was a grown up fully capable of making his own decisions.

"You're not going to scold me. are you?" he said.

"Nope," I answered, "not my place to pass any kind of judgement."

"I'm not a drunk or anything." He began to explain. "I just couldn't seem to stand my life any longer. You ever feel like that?"

"Yeah," I began cautiously, "only I don't choose alcohol to hide behind."

Alex watched me carefully as he placed his teacup on a small table. "What do you use?" His eyes seemed to engulf me.

"I don't know," I hedged and tried not to blush.

"Yes, you do." His voice and posture became commanding. "You know and you've been worrying about it, haven't you?"

"I guess," I began but then I felt very defensive. "Wait a minute. I don't have to deal with this. I get to figure out my own life; not have you do it for me." My voice raised an octave by the time I reached the last word.

"No, no you don't have to deal with it." His voice softened as he turned away. "I just can't help seeing so much of Mother in you. You know you look a lot like her and some of your mannerisms…."

"I'm not her," I screamed as I jumped from the couch. I could not believe my own anger. "I could never be her."

Alex lifted his hands in protest suddenly terrified at the torrent he had unleashed. "Okay, okay," he said and tried to put his arms around me. "I'm sorry. Please don't… I mean, I didn't intend…I'm sorry."

Suddenly he was holding me as I sobbed into his chest. "I'm not her…I'm not. I could never be like that and walk away from people who love me. I can't run into the night and leave people like that."

"I'm sorry, Devon." Alex tried to console me. "I should never have left you. You have been through so much and I know I didn't help by running away."

"I told you, Alex. I'm not going to judge you." I said again as I calmed down, gave up crying and lightly returned his hug. "You are my little brother. I worry about you as a person but I can't say that I would never do the same thing. I just don't want bad things to happen to you."

"Okay," he said as he returned to his chair. Alex began another new subject just a quickly as he had entered into the last one. "How are you feeling? I see your arm is better. I did miss the holidays here, didn't I?"

"Yes." I returned to my place on the couch and reached for the tissues. "I am better and the holiday season is over. Oh, by the way, your grandfather called last week. I told him you were out and I would let you know he had called. I'm not sure whether he was upset about me being here but he really didn't ask who I was. I had given my name when I answered the phone, I think, but he didn't question me." Alex rolled his eyes and made a face at my news.

"I suppose it's not quite like me to be out of touch this time of year. Perhaps I should do something about all that." He seemed to be talking to himself more than me. Alex moved to the phone and dialed.

"Granddad," he began as the connection was made. "It's me, Alex; I just got back from a little Christmas retreat and heard that you had called." This time it was me doing the eye rolling.

"Yes, yes" he continued turning his back toward me, "with Mother's death and all the stress of late, I just sort of took off spur of the moment. So sorry really, didn't mean to worry you." I decided not to stick around to hear what sort of tale he would have to create to explain me. I went into the kitchen and dug around in the cabinets trying to dink some snack to go with the tea in case Alex's guest arrived.

I returned to hear him hang up the phone and we sat quietly contemplating one another for a few minutes until we heard a loud knock at the door. Alex answered it and I watched as he landed a great bear hug with a large man standing in the hallway.

CHAPTER 18
GETTING IT STRAIGHT

We had arrived at Devon's apartment building about half way through her last narrative but sat quietly in the car waiting for her to arrive at this stopping place. Her building was an aging, well kept stucco and brick arrangement just off campus in an older part of town. The sun was bright and the day was quite warm even with the top up but I did not seem to notice. Considering all she had just shared with me; I was truly unsure as to how to proceed.

"Well," Devon said turning slowly to face me, "I suppose I could ask you to come up but that seems awkward considering we just left your place."

"I…I will do whatever you would like." I needed a clear sign from her whether I was to be dismissed or asked to continue listening.

"I sense that something has changed between us." She seemed honestly confused.

"Did you really mean all that you just said about men?" I had to get clear. "I mean about men being gullible and manipulated, is that the way you view me?" I felt very confused and deserved an answer.

"Well, no… or I mean yes…but not like…" she stopped and closed her eyes for a moment. "Freddy" she was talking to me but not looking at me. "I just told you my most intimate thoughts at a very vulnerable time in my life. You wanted to hear my story and I have tried not to leave anything out. Did I expect too much?"

Now it my turn to be embarrassed. "I'm sorry, Devon. I guess I'm just really tired." I reached for her hand but she pulled away.

She opened the car door and stood to face me. Cocking her head to one side she said, "Okay, you are welcome to join me and we can finish this story here or we can put it off until another day or we can call it quits now. We both need sleep but I'm wide awake at the moment. If you decide not to hear the rest, I will have to make you swear to forget you ever heard the first part. I like you; Fred Hanesworthy and I have trusted you with a lot of who I am but…I am a person. I've worked very hard to hide myself from the rest of the human race and done a darn good job of it up to now. Yes, I've been through some crazy stuff but like the waitress at the coffee shop said 'ain't we all."

Devon shut the car door, turned and began walking toward the building. I knew what I was going to do. I wanted to drive away but I would not. I wanted to forget all about her and her life but I could not. She remained enchanting and I was not ready to give up. I threw open my car door and hurried to catch her before she got away. I may have found the building but I really did not know which apartment she inhabited. I caught up with her just as she was starting up a set of stairs inside the lobby area. I slowed down and continued to walk next to her. We did not speak or acknowledge one another until we reached the second floor and were inside her home.

It was very spare in décor; a couch, a chair, a desk with a laptop. No family photos or pieces of art adorned the walls. I saw not evidence of books or even piles of paper or laundry as I had in my home. It appeared that she had indeed just recently moved in and was awaiting the arrival of her things from some other place. She began opening curtains and then windows to let in some fresh air.

"Ah," she said breathing deeply, "springtime in the Midwest, so full of lovely scents and ugly pollen. Hope you don't have any allergies." Our mood lightened as I shook my head.

"Looks like you just moved in." I observed."

"Actually, I did." She answered. "I had an apartment on the other side of the complex last year but when I ended up in the hospital in Africa, Janine and some of the other teachers moved all my stuff to a storage unit close to here. I need to finish clearing things out of there but I just can't seem to find the energy. It's as if I don't know what I want to do with my life next.

We landed together on the sofa and I turned to face her.

"Devon," I took her hand in mine. "May I ask you some pretty direct questions here?"

She pondered a moment before answering. "I suppose you better. I seem to keep saying the wrong things."

"No, not wrong," I said, "just…difficult…at least for me…

to understand."

I looked purposefully into her eyes. "When you started to share this with me earlier this week, I was almost convinced that you would end by telling me how you had found a church or joined a religious group; in other words, a kind of conversion story. Is that where this is leading?"

Again, she stopped to think. "No actually," she answered. "That's sort of the hardest part of all this. Yes, I learned a lot of things about myself. I look or try to look at my life in a new way but I don't think I have necessarily changed that much. Rest assured that I won't be asking you or anyone else to join me in worship any where unless they are curious. I did make the choice to join the Catholic Church but that's not really the point of my life. Maybe I can explain things with the rest of the story.

CHAPTER 19
THE REST

"I am sure you have guessed that the visitor my brother had invited home was Fr. Christian Benoit, the priest I had last seen in Morocco." Devan began. "He was very surprised to see me and we took a few moments sharing where we had been since our last meeting. I don't know who was most surprised me or Alex, that the long-time family friend was also a person I knew. The priest was in London for some meeting when he happened upon Alex in a pub and helped him find his way home. I never did know why a priest was in a pub but I decided to leave well enough alone. We talked about how we were all related and shared the pot of tea along with conversation."

Devon seemed to relax as she talked and I felt more at ease myself.

"Eventually, things got around to the subject of my stay in North Africa and the incident in the desert. I had been rather vague when explaining things to Alex but with Fr. Christian in the room the conversation became more explicit. At one point I even gathered the poetry I had written down from the dreams I had been having and showed it to them. Fr. Christian was pretty impressed by what he read."

"Our conversations went on far into the night. We called for a food delivery. The priest and then my brother questioning and then discussing so many areas of concern in the world. Comparing theology and psychology on each topic they brought up. I would add observations from my field of education in archaeology, which seemed to be quite helpful. Father Christian finally said his goodbyes around three in the morning because he had to catch a flight back to Rome in a couple of hours. Alex and I were worn out and allowed him to leave for the airport unaccompanied. We both went to our rooms and I slept soundly until early the next afternoon."

I decided to begin questioning rather than just listen. "Do you still have the poetry with you?"

"Sure," she said reaching across me and opening a drawer in the table. Her body pressed against mine for only a moment but she was warm and smelled lovely. "I keep them here and actually refer to them almost every day. I kept thinking I would be able to begin writing some of my story down if I reviewed them often enough."

I took the worn sheets she offered and tried to concentrate on the words on the page.

"You know, Devon," I speculated, "some of this is kind of like a prayer maybe. Are these direct quotes of what the woman said in the cave or memories from your dreams about the cave?"

"Truthfully," she said, "they could only be memories of anything. There was no light in the cave when she spoke them. I could hardly have written anything down at that time."

I looked up to find her very close to me on the couch, her gaze concentrated on the page in my hands. I wanted to take her in my arms and kiss her but I remembered our conversation about being a gullible man and decided against it. She had asked me to help her complete a project that felt important and I was determined to stick to business.

"Oh, right." I answered. "Well, they are still quite beautiful. She was obviously a woman well trained in theology. A wise person when it comes to the difficulties of life. These will have to go in the story we write." I placed the pages carefully on the table next to me and turned to face Devon who had once again leaned back against a large pillow behind her. I decided to lean back on my side and reflect her posture rather than lean closer the way I wanted to.

"So, what about the rest of your time in Europe or did you actually stay there?" I asked trying to get my mind back on her story.

"We did travel," she said, "leaving London within a week. Alex and I went to Spain first and then to Italy where we met with Father Benoit again. We spent two weeks around Rome seeing the sights and talking. Everywhere we traveled we found Catholic Churches and at each church or chapel we were able to be part of the celebration of the Mass in the language of that country; seems like we ate and talked and prayed our way across most of Italy. I started to worry that I should be searching for a gym to workout in but I guess being banged up a couple of times kept my weight down."

I had spent enough time around enough women to know not to say anything at this last comment. Devon was very trim but like many American women she had her own set of body image issues. She also seemed to be able to jump from one subject to the next, from one emotion to another without much warning.

"Did you ever get back to your quest for the woman from the cave?" I could see she was not going into depth about conversations at this point.

"Well,", she said, "yes and no. I took a side trip without Alex that led me to the original home of the priest who founded the monastery at Beni Abbes in Africa. Some members of the order are located in France and I was able to obtain a short audience with the Prior of a school they have there. Brother Albert was his name and he told me about the history of his order; something I was already pretty familiar with from my reading. I did not ask him directly about a person who performed miracles and lived forever, being a member of their society. For some reason it was just not that important anymore. I was having weekly conversations with Tanemghurt and even she seemed less concerned. We spoke one more time about the story of Azerwal and I felt she had accepted that there were multiple persons involved. The part about the monk, coming before Islam was probably a tribal legend. The Berber people are still nomads and stay to themselves. They would not have been exposed to new faiths as quickly as those who lived a more settled way of life. There is always exaggeration in myth and sometimes it is not easy for the literal Western mind to understand that. When the few hundred people would gather, the stories would naturally become the biggest, the highest, and the best. The core of the story is always correct but embellishments may have been added."

"You told me you joined the Catholic Church." I said, "Where were you when you did that?"

"Actually," she replied," It was in a small village in the south of France. Father Christian was assigned to be pastor there and it was one of his first services, an Easter Vigil Mass. Tanemghurt and her brother were my godparents and they flew up for the weekend. That was also a good time for us to re-connect."

"Alex was present for the ceremony but he didn't join me in my joy. He was already a member of his Father's church which he attended on an irregular basis with his grandparents. He was all about the psychology of religion and kept making small objections to what I was doing anyway. His friendship with Father Christian went back a few years and was a result of a trip he made to see his dad at one of his mission sites, probably in Morrocco. That was a thing I liked about this priest, he could be friends with people from other faiths and not try to convince them to join his belief system."

"After all of the traveling in Europe," Devon continued, "I flew home and went to try and see my stepmother in Kansas. I got there in time to attend her death and funeral, but I think we already talked about that." Devon became silent again. I waited a few minutes knowing the pain was still recent for her. There were no tears but the sadness registered on her face.

I finally decided to move on. "So, if joining this church is so important to you, why wouldn't you take a friend like me to one of their services?"

"It's not that I wouldn't," she replied, "It's just not the point of the story. I don't think I could be responsible for leading someone else to join any group with just the story of me."

"Why not," I countered, "why couldn't the story of you forgiving a mother who had abandoned and then used you to further her own selfish interests be a vehicle for another person to find comfort in your example?"

"It's not really that simple, Fred." Devon began to fidget in her seat and then rose to pace and then sit again. "There's more to everything than just that."

"Like what" I retorted.

"Like something called forgiving you." She perched first on her chair then back on the sofa, nervously flitting between the two. The physical movement seemed to allow her to concentrate on one subject.

"Forgiving me?" I questioned.

"No, forgiving myself. I know what I have done in my life." She became more agitated with each word. "I know there are people I have offended just as I have felt offended by my mother's actions. Mother almost never asked for forgiveness from me or my brother, but I gave it to her because I had to come to some peace within myself. Now I have to consider those people I have offended in some way. How can I do that if I don't know what it was, I did?"

"I don't understand." I said, "Would this be part of the book?"

"I don't know" she said, "but it was definitely a part of what the Ancient One was telling me in that cave. It is also a part of what I learned in all those months traveling around with Alex, visiting with Father Chistian and talking to Tanemghurt. It's not enough to forgive everyone you've ever met; at some point you have to forgive yourself for the wrongs you have done."

Devon moved very close to me now and placed he hand on my forearm, for the first time I actually saw the scars on her arm, deep red with streaks of white skin like a healed burn. "Freddy, please tell me the truth. What do other people say about me?"

I straightened myself and placed my hand over the scarred place as if to protect the point of perceived pain. "Devon, don't go there. It doesn't matter what other people think of you or me. Sometimes it's even better if we never know."

"Don't they think I'm like my mother? My little brother is an alcoholic who hides behind a bottle and perhaps our mother acted the way she did because of how she felt about herself." Devon looked deeply into my eyes. I had to turn away to answer her and she slipped away from my hand.

"Look" I stammered, "Other people don't know the inside of you. They don't know what motives you. You said yourself that you have spent a great deal of time hiding from the world. How can it possibly matter now?"

"You took the time to ask questions about me, didn't you?" She was still staring into my eyes and I had to turn away again. "I have some idea what you heard and yet you are still here."

I could not come up with a quick answer and she began again as I stammered.

"Perhaps it's not exactly what other people think that I'm looking for here." She said turning away and talking more to herself than to me. "Perhaps it's what I know in my own heart, things that I have done that hurt other people. You were right, Fred. I do think most men are gullible, but I have also believed that all I was good for was sex with them. I don't have any real friends. At least not long-term ones. When it comes to relationships with anyone, I have not valued myself and when they got too close, I did run away. Alex and I had lots of discussions about that subject. We shared a mother so it was easy for him to know how I felt being abandoned as a child. His work in psychology has been in the area of human sexual response and he had tons of things to say about how people act…If I'm going to say anything about my experience it is that I have learned that I am a valuable person and I don't need to manipulate others."

"That is a conversion, Devon." I said the words almost without thinking.

"What?" she replied sharply.

"Well," I scrambled to explain, "sometimes we think of conversions as joining a group or becoming part of a community when in all actuality the word conversion refers to a change of mind or heart. You have taken the words of that woman and applied them to yourself."

"But it wasn't just her words," Devon began to pace, "it was also Tanemghurt and her family and all the stories she told about forgiveness and learning to treat others with respect."

"A lot of this you already knew when you were upset for the way she was treated in her own country." I began to try and help put the pieces of her puzzle together. "You came to the situation in the cave with that American attitude about respect for the individual."

"And what happened in the desert felt so life changing." Devon added. "Alex helped me understand that how I value myself becomes how I value others. We decided that the knowledge about how our mother acted should become a necessary part of learning to deal with our own lives."

"So, what about me?" I asked.

"What do you mean?" she asked whirling to look at me.

"You think I'm not worthy of respect, don't you?" I looked directly at her almost defiant.

Devon wrinkled her brow in thought and returned to sit next to me on the sofa. "Fred, I don't disrespect you. I want to be your friend even if we never write this down. Why would I trust you with my story if I thought that way?"

"What about the 'oh Freddy, don't leave me alone' line? Wasn't that just a little bit manipulative?" I wanted to be angry but didn't feel that way.

"I guess old habits are hard to break but didn't you accept it at the time?" Devon countered. "Besides, you haven't stayed with me just because I tell a good story, have you?" She wasn't teasing, she was taunting and she was not wrong. I blushed a bit and breathed a small laugh.

"Well, okay." I had to admit. "But that still does not address how you feel about me as a man. Why did you pick me to tell this to instead of, oh I don't know, maybe the Andersens? Why not confide in a good girlfriend from the English department, if you really want to write a book?"

She let out a long sigh. "Maybe because I don't have a girlfriend? Didn't Helen ever talk to you about why we were not great friends?" I shook my head and leaned toward her. "When she and I roomed together, I actually went out of my way to steal a boyfriend from her. It was before she met you, I'm sure; but I just did it to be…I don't know…I don't even remember that much about him. I just remember the huge fight she and I had and how awful I felt after it was over. I never told her and now it seems so long ago…I suppose I could come up with a lot of excuses but they won't mean much between us. Some parts of this whole thing are so hard. I can see that I have used people who wanted to be part of my life so they went away, or I pushed them away."

"You…ah…you haven't given up on sex altogether, have you?" My question was purely personal. "I mean, you weren't planning on joining…I've heard the Catholics have these rules about sex and…"

"No, no" she laughed a little brightening her appearance. "I just intend to be more respectful of the gift God has given us in that part of our humanity. Maybe that's really the other part or even the biggest part of all this." Devon quieted down to explain. "It's putting God in the middle of the view of things that made the really big difference. For all of my life I have lived as if there might not be God but after these experiences, I know there is. If there were no God, I would have continued the journey of my life without recognizing the need for forgiveness. It's the quality that Jesus brought and modeled for us in such an exquisite way. I can get very caught up in my feelings of sorrow and loss but when I reflect on what I have learned about God and Jesus Christ I can sort of slide past that and look at a larger more complex picture."

"And again, I will say," I replied, "why would all this not be something to share with others? After all wasn't there a wise woman in the desert who cautioned you to be careful of your judgements since you never know who God will pick?"

Devon smiled quietly. "I think you are right; I am sharing this with a friend and I am sorry for giving the impression that I don't respect you. I still haven't figured out why all this even happened to me. Most of these conversion moments seem to be for people who are searching for something in their lives and I don't believe I was searching for anything more that artifacts when I ended up in that cave."

"So why did you choose to become a Catholic?" I asked. "Was that priest so wise and charismatic that you wanted to follow him?"

"No," Devon smiled as she remembered him. "Father Benoit is smart and very open but I joined the Church as a way to exercise the faith that I was feeling. Once I had processed that cave experience and questioned the irrationality of it, I began to believe that a greater Being was behind it all. It's like when you read poetry; the author might have had a specific meaning in mind but it is what speaks to your heart that stays with you."

"You know you are a different person than the Devon I remember." I said without looking at her. I knew we were reaching an intimate place.

"Maybe Tanemghurt was wrong," Devon said. "Maybe God does heal people without their asking. I've been sort of broken on some deeply personal levels for a long time and just could not admit it. Maybe God wanted to heal that. I feel like I can be a real friend now."

We were together on the sofa again. I put my hand on her shoulder and pulled her face so that I might look directly into her eyes. "I think I can be your friend, maybe not for ever but for now."

Devon and I are caught in one another's lives as friends. We decided to make good use of the laptop in her apartment and jot down the major events as they had occurred. From this humble beginning we have created this small tale about a large life. However, I have opted to share the story only from my own perspective as this is the one I know best. I would tell you how it all ended but I have not reached that point. We continue to see one another and I continue to be enchanted.

Along with that enchantment has come a questioning of my own life. I had recognized that I was searching for something more in the life I was living the day I met up with her. That will be one of my own days to remember. Was Devon the answer to my life of loneliness? Was she the recipient of some great biological healing? Did it all really matter in the end? Was belonging to a church group the end of a life's journey? Was one better than another? It is a conundrum, and one wrestled with by far greater minds than my own.

CHAPTER 20
GETTING IT STRAIGHT

Sitting here in my car at the airport in the pickup line, reflecting on the story of the one I am coming to see as the love of my life. Devon has entered the terminal to wait for her brother, Alex, and their friend, Tanemghurt. I'm still not sure how they managed to get on the same flight out of New York but we are quite grateful that they did. One less trip in killer traffic for us. It has been just ten days since I began to hear about the adventures of Devon. I'm still not sure I can take it all in. Devon and two people exit the terminal and begin to load luggage in the trunk of her car so I jump out to help. We need to move quickly as there is a line of cars waiting behind us.

The sound of jet engines roaring and traffic moving drowns out any chance for conversation. Smiles and nods are all that I can manage. I had never seen Tanemghurt and her appearance was unexpected. She is quite small in comparison to the rest of us, her complexion rather dark but very beautiful. Alex on the other hand, I could easily pick out in a crowd. He is tall, lanky, and has the exact same eyes as his sister.

The ride to Devon's apartment is all chit chat and introductions. How was your flight and did you get any rest on the airplane? They both answered in the affirmative and seemed quite ready to jump into a new experience. I was driving and Devon suggests we at least drive past the university on the way home. Tanemghurt seems quite excited by the idea and the two ladies begin to talk and compare notes about first this person and then another. Alex remained quite silent, smiling and nodding at his sister and then at me in the rear-view mirror. I was able to concentrate on the traffic so my conversational contact was limited at best.

Arriving at Devon's apartment, we went in to refresh a bit and discuss our housing arrangements. Devon had wanted both of them to stay with her but she only has a one-bedroom flat with a pull-out couch. I offered my two-bedroom apartment but Alex announced that he much preferred checking into a hotel near the campus. He had made some connections with a couple of professors in the psychology department and shared that he would feel more comfortable if he could come and go as he pleased. I looked at Devon and shrugged my shoulders and she returned a nod.

Restrooms were pointed out and Devon went into the kitchen to make tea. It was mid-afternoon and the usual time for such a repast. We all began to settle in around her small dining table. Silence had floated frostily in the air for a few minutes.

"Professor," Tanemghurt spoke, "there is a church near here? It is soon to be Sunday and I would very much like to attend the Mass.'

"Oh, yes, Tanemghurt," she began to pour the tea and offer the small cookies. "I usually attend the 10:00 a.m. Mass on Sunday morning and you are certainly welcome to come with me. It's a very pretty chapel on campus. Very simple in some ways." I had actually never noticed this chapel but then, I may have passed it off as some other office or slightly ornate teaching hall. Alex indicated that he would not care to join the ladies as he was as he said 'in flux' about the religion thing.

"Perhaps you ladies would like to know what I found out about your holy person." Alex gave a smug look to his sister as we all held our breath. We knew he wasn't in agreement with those at the table who believed that miracles had occurred. I wasn't sure he knew that Devon had gone alone to search for the person she had encountered in the dark of the cave.

As soon as Devon had left to return to the United States, Alex began to search in earnest for the religious group that Tanemghurt and Fadil had told him about. They had shared what they knew including a few folk tales about the mysterious person who taught and healed people in the desert.

Alex had set out to disprove the apparition's existence; to find some logical, human explanation for the person as well as the healing that was attributed to him or her. Devon said nothing as her younger brother developed his tale. He left London and went first to Morocco and then to the village where Tanemghurt lived. He did not have an address for the family but was able to track down the place in the desert where the encampment had been the year before. At first, he assumed that there would be no gathering because the individual had died or been horribly injured, but he was wrong. Waiting around in the village, Alex began to hear about the gathering to come. This year would be larger than ever since there had been another great miracle.

Unable to obtain an invitation to the gathering, he flew next to the city where the priestly order maintained a permanent residence in Algeria. At no time had he heard a name for the individual who had been in the cave with his sister but he felt sure that the abbey would know where its members went each year. Upon arrival at the residence, he was escorted into an office and introduced to Father Lawrence, the head of the group. He was not recognizable to Alex as more than an ordinary business man. He wore a casual shirt and slacks; no roman collar and no black dress.

After sharing tea and polite conversation, Alex began to reveal the true reason for his visit. The priest began to visibly stiffen as he explained his mission to find the individual who had been trapped in a cave last year. He shared that his sister had been in the cave, was saved and was very well. He wanted the priest to understand that he only wanted to personally thank the person for helping his family.

The priest, who spoke very good English, seemed disquieted by the request. There was a rather long silence before he finally spoke.

"May I ask," the priest began, "are you Catholic?"

"No," Alex was confused by this line of questioning.

"Are you a member of a Christian organization?" he continued.

"Well," Alex grew uncomfortable, "my father is an Anglican missionary but I can't say that I…"

"So" the priest continued, "your concern comes from your training as a child to know your father's teaching?"

"No" Alex answered, "my concern comes from my training as a psychologist wanting to understand what exactly happened in that cave."

"We do not enjoy curiosity seekers." The priest appeared to be irritated at Alex. "Perhaps you want to expose the person who was in the desert accident. Perhaps you want to sell your 'news' to some papers for their exclusive expose."

"No" Alex was nearly shouting.

"The other person in that cave," the priest began, "was a young Berber girl. You are obviously not her brother. What is it you truly want. Are you an insurance investigator?"

Alex drew back in his chair. "I guess I don't want anything. I believe I will leave now."

Both men rose and Alex headed for the door. This was most

disconcerting. Why was it so secret? What actually happened in that desert? He would return to the desert but this time in search of the one man who might share the truth with him; Azerwal. His search began in Tanemghurt's village and led him to her families' home. Tanemghrut herself welcomed him and was delighted to see her friend's family at her door.

Through Tanemghurt and her family he was able to make an appointment to see the aging leader Azerwal. They did not travel as far into the desert as the encampment as the elderly gentleman was quite ill and lay in a family tent at the edge of the town, being tended by distant relatives. Alex knew he did not wish to tire the man but he had a very deep need to know and the story his sister told pointed to this man as the holder of great knowledge.

"What is it you really wish to know, my son?" The old man wheezed the question.

"I would like to know who the person was that saved my sister's life." It seemed a reasonable request to Alex.

Azerwal smiled wearily and turned away. "You wish to know if this was a priest? You wish to know if the person was Catholic or Muslim? You wish to know if there really was a miracle because the saving of your sister doesn't sound like a miracle to you?"

"Well, I..." Alex felt ill at ease.

"Well, a holy miracle can be many different things. Sometimes it is a healing of illness and sometimes it is a return to life in a way that changes a man's attitude." Azerwal turned and looked deeply at Alex as if he were trying to see inside his very soul. "What is it you are running away from, my son?"

Alex felt stunned and tongue-tied. He thought he wanted a definitive answer to a simple question, instead he saw displayed a series of choices. Some small and others difficult. Most of equal value.

"You are a lonely man." The ancient one announced. "You try to hold people away by finding fault with their philosophy. Perhaps you think others hold some key to life. We each hold the key to our own life. The hard part is letting the Holy Spirit in. Perhaps that is the miracle."

'But what about this 'miracle' the people thought they saw." Alex gained his voice. "Did this Holy person float out of a hole in desert and heal a young woman's arm?"

Azerwal shrugged his shoulders, "I don't know. The person came out of the cave, yes. The young woman's arm was not broken after three days in the dark. Why can you not accept that other people want to believe in miracles? The question is – are these people better human beings once they have been part of this 'miracle'?

Alex listened for another hour as the dying man continued to pour out his knowledge and philosophy. Sometimes it made immediate sense but most of what he heard would be stored away to consider and ruminate on as he traveled back to Europe. Along the way he would convince Tanemghurt to join him. They stopped in London long enough to give his traveling companion a glimpse of the England Alex enjoyed.

Plans began to form that Tanemghurt would restart her education at the university where she already knew a few friends and perhaps, Alex would join them. The secrets each learned would remain in the desert.